BUSHWACKED IN BED!

From under the bed he saw the legs of the four out-laws as they pulled up in front of the bed and poured lead into it. Longarm cut loose himself, and saw one man stagger and go down. As the other three turned and bolted from the room, a stick of dynamite struck the floor and rolled toward him, its fuse sparkling like a Chinese firecracker. . . .

*   *   *

SPECIAL PREVIEW!

Turn to the back of this book for a sneak-peek excerpt from the exciting, brand new Western series . . .

FURY

. . . **the blazing story of a gunfighting legend.**

TABOR EVANS

LONGARM

AND THE CHEYENNE KID

JOVE BOOKS, NEW YORK

LONGARM AND THE CHEYENNE KID

A Jove Book / published by arrangement with
the author

PRINTING HISTORY
Jove edition / August 1992

ISBN: 0-515-10901-0

Jove Books are published by The Berkley Publishing Group,
200 Madison Avenue, New York, New York 10016.
The name "JOVE" and the "J" logo
are trademarks belonging to Jove Publications, Inc.

PRINTED IN THE UNITED STATES OF AMERICA

10   9   8   7   6   5   4   3   2   1

Chapter 1

Longarm sat quietly beside Town Marshal Sam Calder on the veranda of Summit's only hotel. The two men had tipped their chairs back against the wall, their booted feet resting on the veranda railing. Across the street squatted the Wells Fargo express office. Summit was a gold-mining town high in Idaho's snow-tipped peaks, and its main street was nearly empty as the pitiless midsummer sun poured down on it and on the raw, unpainted buildings fronting it.

A big man, spooky tall, still on the comfortable side of forty, Custis Long was a lean, muscular giant with the body of a young athlete. The raw sun and winds he'd ridden through had cured his rawboned features to a saddle-leather brown. Were it not for the gunmetal blue of his wide-set eyes and the tobacco-leaf color of his close-cropped hair, he could have been mistaken for an Indian. He had a flaring longhorn mustache, and wore his snuff-brown Stetson dead center, tilted slightly forward cavalry style, its crown telescoped in the fashion of a Colorado rider.

At the moment the two men were discussing the preposterous adventures of Dead Eye Dick, a hero in a few of Erasmus Beadle's dime novels, too many of which littered the hotel lobby behind them.

"Hard to believe anyone would believe that crap," remarked Calder, shaking his head in pure wonderment.

The town marshal wore a black Stetson, a clean white cotton shirt under his vest, and faded Levi's tucked into scuffed half boots. He looked to be close to Longarm's age and had a crooked tilt to his wide shoulders. A black patch covered his right eye, and from the socket trailed a long, puckered scar that ran clear back to his right ear, imparting to that side of his face an odd, squinty look. He was, as everyone in town agreed wholeheartedly, an ugly-looking son of a bitch.

"Well," Longarm reminded him, "to some people, fiction seems a damn sight more real than life."

"Even when it don't make no sense? When it ain't even logical?"

"You mean you didn't believe it," Longarm drawled, "when you read how Grizzly Bill killed that grizzly bear with a kitchen knife?"

"Laugh all you want, Longarm," Calder said, a serious cast to his broken face, "but these crazy stories encourage young punks to leave their wives and children, buy shiny new Colts and cowboy suits in St. Louis, then come out here to make their fame and fortune."

"That's a problem, all right," Longarm conceded. "Seems like them fool writers back East end up inventing the Wild West for us."

2

"And we got to handle the mess that results."

Longarm chuckled. He had to admit it. Sam was right.

Leaning back, he inhaled on his cheroot. It was a damn fool habit, he realized, one he had been trying to quit for some time. Well . . . he'd think about that some other time.

It was the first time in the past three weeks that Longarm had been able to relax. Billy Vail had sent him up here to haul in Len Turco, a hapless would-be train robber who'd blown up a baggage car, killing the postal employee and a federal marshal, while making such a botch of things that he'd also blown to smithereens the safe and the money along with the car. No one had seen the crazy dynamiter since. Longarm had come up here following a tip that Turco was riding with a local gang. But after two weeks of combing this high country, Longarm had drawn a blank—and now he was waiting for the stage to take him back home, empty-handed, to the Mile High City.

His wait these past two days for the stage had been lightened considerably by the chance this delay gave him to visit with his old saddle buddy. Longarm had known Sam Calder since he first came West. The two had done some cowpunching together, and for a while Longarm and Sam had served as town marshal and deputy of a mining town in the western reaches of Colorado, an assignment that had bored both of them silly. Five years ago the two had parted company. This was their first get-together since. Longarm had found his laconic friend unchanged and as ugly-looking as ever. His appearance was fearsome and lent credence to the rumor that it was the result of a bare-handed struggle with an enraged grizzly, a rumor Sam did nothing to dispel. The truth was Sam had fallen from a moving freight train, and it was Longarm who'd leaped off the train after him, then carried him on his back to a sawbones who'd put Calder's broken shoulder and torn face back together as best he could.

Longarm lit another cheroot.

As he looked up from his cupped hands and tossed away his match, he noticed four men in gray dust-slickers, hat brims shading their faces, crossing the street, heading for the steps leading up to the Wells Fargo loading platform. Glancing further up the street, he caught sight of a fifth man, also in a dust-slicker, riding toward them on a gray gelding. He was leading four saddled mounts.

"You see what I see?" Longarm asked.

"Yep," said Calder. "I see 'em."

"You thinkin' what I'm thinkin'?"

"Yep."

Calder pushed his chair gently forward. The front legs came down on the porch soundlessly. Calder stood up. Longarm flicked his just-lighted cheroot into the street and eased his chair forward also, but he remained seated as the fifth outlaw continued toward them, leading the four horses the rest of his gang would need for their escape.

"Stay here and keep your ass down," Calder told him. "This is my town. Ain't no reason for you to get involved."

He removed the marshal's badge from his vest and dropped it into his pocket. Longarm understood. Calder

4

wanted to get across the street and into that express office behind those four men without alerting the one in the street that he was the law.

"I'll go with you."

"No need, Longarm."

"Hell, there's four of them. You need to cut the odds."

"You keep an eye on that jasper bringin' the horses," he said. "I'll go inside here and get Red."

Calder ducked past Longarm back into the hotel, and emerged a moment later with his deputy at his side. Red was a young redhead that Calder insisted was as tough as a smithy's nail. Snugging his hat down firmly, Calder descended the hotel steps with Red and headed for the Wells Fargo office. Longarm watched them go for a moment or two, then got to his feet as casually as he could and followed after the two men. Calder was his friend, which meant he didn't see that he needed any special invite to deal himself in.

Gaining the wooden sidewalk on the other side of the street, Longarm kept a good five paces behind Calder and Red. When they entered the Wells Fargo office, Longarm stepped into a doorway and waited, his eye on the mounted outlaw bringing up the four mounts. For long minutes there was no sound from inside the express office. The mounted outlaw rode closer. Longarm rested his right hand on the walnut grips of his double-action Colt.

Then all hell broke loose.

From inside the express office came the crash of gunfire. The four outlaws burst from the office and bolted down the steps, guns drawn as they peered about for targets of opportunity. Longarm stepped out of the doorway and fired on the fifth outlaw, to prevent him from bringing the horses any closer. He caught the man in the chest, but the fellow leaned forward over the saddlehorn and spurred on to the express office. He dropped the reins of the saddled horses, then kept on past it down the street. Saddlebags slung over their shoulders, the four outlaws raced out into the street, grabbed up the trailing reins of their horses, and swung aboard.

Longarm got off two quick shots. One outlaw peeled off his mount, while the rest of them sent a concentrated salvo at him as they spurred past. Ducking low, Longarm got off one more shot, and saw another rider grab his shoulder and almost tumble from his saddle. Longarm got a good look at one of the other outlaws. He had close-set eyes, a long snout, and a receding chin, fitting perfectly the description Billy Vail had given him of Len Turco.

Before he could track Turco with his .44, a slug caught him in his left side, spinning him about in the doorway. There was no immediate pain. It felt as if someone had punched him. He flung himself out into the street and in a bitter, futile gesture, emptied his .44 at the fleeing outlaws. Before he could reload, they had vanished into the dust they raised as they galloped out of town.

Ignoring the heavy slick of blood encasing his left thigh, Longarm hurried up the steps into the express office and found the deputy dead on the floor beside the potbelly stove, his face shattered by a bullet. On the floor in front of the counter Sam Calder was lying in a pool of his own blood, his one eye shut, a distraught Wells Fargo clerk bending over him. The clerk looked up as Longarm approached.

"How bad is he?" Longarm asked.

The clerk shook his head doubtfully.

Longarm went down on one knee beside his old friend, berating himself. He should have gone in with Calder. As he had pointed out to him, it would have cut the odds.

He pulled back the skirt of Calder's frock coat and found a gaping hole in the man's gut, pieces of slick, gray intestines poking out through the hole. With each breath he took, Calder's intestines inched out still further. Calder opened his eye and peered up at Longarm.

"Shit, Longarm," he gasped painfully. "I'm gutshot!"

"Don't move. Stay quiet," Longarm told him.

"What about Red?"

"He took a bullet in the head. He's gone."

"Jesus. I really blew it, Longarm."

"I should've come in with you."

"No. You would've bought it too. It's my fault. All my fault."

"Quiet. Just stay quiet."

By this time miners and townsmen were crowding into the express office, those behind jostling those in front in an effort to get a better view of the bloodied law officers. Longarm looked up and saw the doctor, using his black bag as a battering ram, pushing his way through their ranks. A quick inspection of Red told him all he needed to know. Then he brushed Longarm to one side and examined Calder's wound.

He glanced up at the four closest onlookers and told them to carry the wounded marshal over to the saloon. He would have to operate on the bar. Longarm followed at a distance, limping painfully. The numbness had worn

7

off by now to be replaced by a sharp, nagging pain. In addition, most of his left side was now encased in a heavy carapace of blood.

But right now, Longarm realized, the doctor had a patient to look after who was in far worse condition.

Later that night, his flesh wound sewn up by the doc, Longarm sat a lonely vigil beside Sam Calder as he lay unconscious on his bed. Calder did not look good. His color had faded completely. The eye patch had been taken off by the doctor and no one had bothered to replace it. Though the doctor had shoved Calder's intestines back into his abdomen and sewn him back up, the man held little hope for the marshal's survival. He had already told Longarm that Calder would be lucky if he lasted through the night.

Calder stirred. Longarm leaned close.

"Water," Calder whispered hoarsely.

Longarm filled a glass from a pitcher sitting on the night table and lifted Calder's head so he could drink from it. Calder gulped the water greedily, then coughed most of it back up.

Longarm put the glass down. "What happened in there, Sam?"

Calder shook his head slightly. "I was such a fool, Longarm," he whispered. "Such a damn fool!"

Longarm placed a restraining hand on Calder's arm. "No need to get riled. Just tell me what happened."

"Son of a bitch," he said, his voice hoarse. "It was the Cheyenne Kid who gutshot me."

"Cheyenne?"

Calder nodded. "That's right. My old sidekick."

"You mean you rode with him?"

"A few years ago. I ain't proud of it."

"And he shot you?"

"I walked in there and saw Cheyenne," Calder whispered. "I was surprised. I tell you, Longarm, it really stopped me. I didn't keep my gun on them. I let it drop. Cheyenne smiled. He seemed real glad to see me."

"Then he shot you."

"I didn't expect it. One minute he was smiling, coming toward me like I was his long-lost brother; the next moment he was pumping a slug into me. It happened so fast, I never had a chance to fire back." He let his head fall back on the pillow and closed his eye. "Poor Red. He never had a chance."

"I think I recognized one of the gang, Sam. I think it's that jasper I came up here to bring in. Len Turco. You got any idea where Cheyenne might be headin'?"

"For the past couple of months I been hearing . . . things. There's a near-abandoned town in the mountains . . . north of here."

Longarm leaned closer. "Where?"

"Big Rock . . . Lost River Range."

Longarm sat back. He knew the Lost River country. But he had never heard of Big Rock.

"I heard shots outside," Calder said.

"That was me."

"How many of them did you get?"

"I killed one of them and winged two others. The rest got away."

"You goin' after them?"

"Looks like it."

"Get that bastard Cheyenne for me."

"Sure, Sam," Longarm replied. "But I ain't goin' alone. You'll be ridin' right alongside me when we overtake them bastards. The doc's taken out the Kid's slug and he's sewn you up as neat as a Thanksgiving turkey."

"You're a lousy liar, Longarm. I ain't goin' nowhere."

"Hell, you ain't."

"Now that you mention it, Longarm. That might be just where I'm headed."

"Don't talk like that."

Sam smiled faintly up at Longarm and reaching out, rested his hand on Longarm's wrist. Abruptly, his smile became a grimace. He gasped and closed his eye, writhing on the bed like a stomped worm. His broken face seemed to cave in, his long body ceased its struggle and stretched out; a kind of sigh escaped his lips. The struggle had been a brief one, and when it was over Sam Calder had given up his ghost.

Longarm stood up and looked down at the man who had lowered his gun at sight of an old comrade—and been rewarded with a hot slug in his gut. He drew the sheet up over Sam Calder's face and left the room.

Chapter 2

Close to sundown a week later, Longarm rode into Big Rock, his hat brim low enough to shield his eyes from the sun's straight-on glare. The town was a huddle of unpainted, weathered buildings crouched amid the towering peaks of the Lost River Range. A plank bridge carried him over the creek and into the town. For a dispiriting while he rode beside empty single-story wood-frame houses, their dust-laden, curtainless windows staring spookily out at him. Soon he came to the business district, false-fronted buildings crowding both sides of a narrow, rutted street. An intersection loomed. On its four corners sat a hotel, a general store, a boarded-up saloon, and a livery stable. The stable was still in business, and he dismounted in front of it. A white-haired old man materialized out of its gloom, pitchfork in hand.

"First stall on the right," he told Longarm.

Longarm gave his black a drink at the trough first, then led it into the stall, where he removed its saddle and wiped off the gum that had formed under the saddle blanket. He told the stable owner to grain the black, and lugged his gear across the street to the hotel. A hand-lettered sign advertised a room in back with tubs. After he checked out his room and dumped his gear onto the bed, he went back downstairs and took advantage of the big corrugated steel bathtubs. Feeling ten pounds lighter, he took his supper in the hotel's cramped dining room. Then he drifted through the hotel lobby into its attached saloon—evidently the only watering hole left in town.

He purchased a whiskey and took it over to a small table near the wall and sat down. For a town that appeared on the surface to be stone-cold dead, there was considerable activity. The batwings were seldom still. Most of these newcomers had the look of men on the dodge. The saloon grew noisier by the minute, and soon a squadron of six-percentage girls made their appearance, too many of them exhibiting the world-weary, mechanical smiles of women who had long since given up on real emotion.

There was one exception, an olive-skinned Mexican girl with gleaming teeth and long black hair. Her name was Rita and he heard it called out more than once as she worked. Like the other bar girls, she wore a bright red dress with torn bangles, the bodice low enough to give a generous view of her ample cleft, the skirt's hem just high enough to show off her ankles. She was taller than the other girls and was filled out in all the right places. She seemed quite popular—though it was obvious she was determined to keep strictly to business, which meant serving drinks to the customers, tickling a few under the chin, then scooting swiftly off to serve others. In this fashion, keeping constantly on the move, she escaped most of the pawing and indignities the other girls were forced to endure.

Longarm had spent a long weary day in the saddle, and the scene before him made him wearier by the minute. He finished his whiskey, stood up and stretched, then walked back into the hotel lobby to get his room key. As the clerk handed it to him, Longarm heard a sharp scuffle behind him. He spun around to see the Mexican bar girl being hauled roughly into the hotel lobby by two unkempt older men, their yellow teeth gleaming wolfishly through their tobacco-stained beards.

At once a fat man—evidently the hotel owner—rushed out from behind the front desk and planted himself squarely between the two men and the stairs.

"Where you takin' Rita?" he demanded.

"You mean you don't know?" said the one holding the girl's wrist.

"Hey, Bingham," said his grinning companion. "What's the fuss? We got a room upstairs. We already paid for it."

Longarm looked the two men over. They were obviously just in off the trail, their boots dirt-encrusted, their faces and hands black from lack of soap and water. They stank worse than the horses they rode in on. The one who still held Rita's wrist was the taller—a lean, raw-faced saddle tramp with narrow, squinting eyes. His companion was smaller, hunched over, with sick yellow eyes that matched his few remaining teeth.

"Now, look here, Bingham," the raw-faced one told the hotel owner, "Rick and me, we're sick of playin' grab-ass. So we'll be taking this here sweetie upstairs to play with all by ourselves. She's got enough for both of us!"

"No, Pete," insisted Bingham. "Rita is not like the other girls."

"That's why we're takin' her."

"Look," said Bingham. "Go back in the saloon. I'll bring you Louise. She'll be right down. She just got in from St. Louis. She's our French lady. You will have a fine time with her, believe me."

"Now, listen, Bingham," Pete told the owner heavily. "It's Rita we want, not some clapped-up whore from St. Louis."

"No!" insisted Bingham.

Rick laughed. "Hey, you ain't trying to keep Rita for yourself, are you?"

Bingham was obviously close to desperation. "Gentlemen! Please! I promised her parents I would take good care of her. She is like my own daughter."

Ignoring Bingham, Rick yanked Rita closer to the stairs. Longarm saw the girl grimace as his hard fingers closed viselike about her wrist. The girl dug in her heels, refusing to follow him. He yanked her arm, and this time the pain was such she uttered a tiny cry.

Longarm dropped his room key into his side pocket, caught the girl's eye, and winked. It was not a playful wink, but one designed to alert the girl to his intentions. The look in her eyes told him she comprehended instantly. Longarm moved ahead of the two men, gently nudged Bingham aside, and positioned himself at the foot of the stairs.

"Hey, Rita," he cried, ignoring the other two. "Where you goin'? I just rode in. I'd told you I'd meet you here tonight. How come you're with these two animals?"

"Hey," protested Rick. "Who're you, mister?"

"Dead Eye Dick," Longarm told him. "Dead Eye to my friends. And you better let go of Rita."

"I will like hell."

With a quick, downward swipe of his arm, Longarm slammed the blade of his right hand against Rick's wrist. Rick cried out, grabbed his wrist, and jumped back, releasing Rita's hand as he did so. Longarm grinned at him and drew Rita close to him, one arm about her waist. He whispered to her to play along.

"Why, Dead Eye," she cried, more than equal to the task. "Where have you been? I've been waiting for you."

"Wait no longer, Rita girl. Here I am!"

Longarm caught the hotel owner's eye and winked. The man quickly hurried back behind the front desk, obviously relieved that Longarm had stepped in. Longarm swung Rita gently past him, patted her on the ass, and sent her up the stairs ahead of him, then followed after her.

But Pete and Rick would have none of it.

Overtaking Longarm halfway up the stairs, Pete grabbed Longarm from behind and spun him about. Rick was right behind him.

"You ain't foolin' us, you son of a bitch!" Pete cried, furious. "You're just stickin' your nose in to get Rita for yourself!"

"You sure of that?"

"We saw her first," said Pete.

"Go back into the saloon and cool off," Longarm advised.

"Now listen, you meddlin' son of a bitch, we—"

Pete never got the rest of it out. Longarm slapped him in the chops, sending him ass-over-teakettle back down the stairs. Rick clawed for his six-gun. But before he could get his own gun up, he found himself staring into the yawning bore of Longarm's gun. As Rick lowered his gun, sweat broke out on his forehead. At the foot of the stairs Pete reached for his own gun. Longarm darted down the stairs and knocked the gun out of Pete's hand with a single swipe of his .44. With a startled yelp Pete ducked back away from Longarm, holding his hand.

"Watch out!" cried Rita.

He swung around as Rick charged down the stairs at him. Longarm ducked aside and caught the man with both hands as he rushed past him. Increasing Rick's momentum, he propelled him headfirst into the wall. The wall appeared to bend under the impact of Rick's skull. Rick shook himself groggily, then turned and lunged drunkenly at Longarm. Longarm waited patiently, grabbed him by the back of his shirt, spun him around, then booted him back through the batwings into the saloon. He heard the sound of a table overturning as Rick crashed to the floor. A high-pitched scream followed from one of the bar girls, after which there was a sudden, awesome silence. Longarm waited for Rick to pick himself up and reappear in the doorway. But Rick remained in the saloon and Longarm turned around to attend to Pete. Pete, holding onto his swollen hand, made no effort to continue the argument.

Longarm looked up the stairs at Rita. "Go on up," he told her.

She turned and hurried up the stairs, and with a pleasant nod to Bingham and the desk clerk trembling beside him, Longarm followed Rita up the stairs. They entered his room together.

As Longarm closed the door, Rita turned to him, her face radiant with gratitude.

"Thank you, *señor*," she cried. "You save me from those peegs! You are so brave!"

"I was glad to help, Rita," Longarm assured her. "But don't worry. I won't keep you long." He moved past her to the bed and sank wearily down onto it. "Just stay in here for a while—until those two find someone else to amuse them. Maybe the French lady. Who are they anyway?"

"They have a mine somewhere in the mountains. They get a little gold dust from it, but not much. It is well hidden. I hear they have killed a few who stumbled on it."

Longarm frowned suddenly, aware of a growing discomfort in his side. He felt it gingerly, and reckoned he must have opened up the flesh wound slightly. The wound was warm and heavy with fresh blood. The stitches might have ripped out during that sudden flurry of activity downstairs.

"Excuse me, Rita," he said, carefully shrugging out of his shirt. "But I think I'm going to have to lie back and rest up."

As he flung the shirt onto the back of a chair, he exposed the blood-soaked bandage just above the belt line. Rita uttered a cry and hurried to Longarm's side. Kneeling beside the bed to get a better view, she began to unwind the dressing slowly as Longarm leaned back

17

against the headboard. Her fingers were deft and gentle. When she removed the bandage, Longarm looked closely at the wound and felt considerably relieved. Though a great deal of blood had oozed through the sutures, they appeared to be holding. Rita got to her feet.

"I come back soon," she told him. "You stay quiet, please."

Longarm was in no mood to argue. He placed his Colt under his pillow, then lay back full length on the bed, his head resting on it. Rita hurried from the room, returning a short while later with a pan of steaming water, fresh bandages, and an enormous bar of yellow soap.

"I will clean the stitches," she announced, setting the pan down on a night table.

"With that bar of soap?"

"You will see. It will do good job."

Longarm grinned at her. "Okay, do your worst."

"You mean my best, Dead Eye Dick."

He grinned at her as she began scrubbing gently at the scabbed stitches. "That's not my name, Rita. It's Long. Custis Long."

"I did not think you had such a silly name," she said, smiling brilliantly back at him. "So now I call you Custis?"

"Only when we're alone."

She smiled back at him again, then bent intently over his wound, her soap-laden washcloth gentle but efficient. He could feel a slight sting as the yellow soap sank in past the stitches, but that fact comforted him. When a few minutes later she wound a fresh bandage around his midsection, she did so firmly, leaving him with a bandage that was supportive—yet not unduly tight.

18

Gingerly, Longarm probed the area about the wound. It felt better already. He leaned back and smiled gratefully at Rita.

"Very good, Rita. Thanks. Feels a lot better."

Pleased, she pulled off his boots, then began unbuttoning his fly. He started to tell her he was too tired for play, but caught himself in time and let her deft fingers peel his pants off him. In a moment he lay naked on the bed before her. She reached out and ran her fingers along the powerful, ridged muscles standing out on his chest and shoulders; then she stepped swiftly out of her skirt. Her chemise and slip went next, and she stood before him naked, her long dark hair flowing down past her buttocks, her pubic patch gleaming darkly.

"I want you to understand, Rita," Longarm told her, feeling the quickening in his loins. "I did not take you from those two so I could have you for myself. I just wanted to help."

"I know that, Custis," she said, gazing over his powerful figure. "But you must see how it is for me."

"What do you mean?"

"You have all your teeth. You have shoulders as wide as a barn door. You do not smell like the horse manure, and you have eyes as blue as lake water. Besides, you are one fine gentleman." She joined him eagerly on the bed and snuggled close to him, her hand dropping slyly to his crotch. "So now I thank you for helping me—and reward myself too."

Easing her silken body up on top of him, she slipped her long legs over his torso. He kissed her on her warm, responsive lips, then fastened his mouth to her breasts,

19

his tongue flicking at her erect nipples while his big hand explored her completely, gently.

Only when at last she began to moan aloud and grabbed a fistful of his hair, threatening to scalp him without the benefit of a knife, did he roll her slowly over. One knee spread her thighs as he eased himself up onto her. He teased her entrance with the tip of his erection.

"You are devil," Rita gasped. "You drive this woman wild! Please! Do not play with me any longer."

He smiled down at her. "I'll see what I can do."

He plunged in. So moist had she become as a result of his foreplay, he could barely feel the walls of her muff closing about his erection. But she remedied matters promptly and her inner muscles tightened on him like a powerful fist. He felt himself swell magnificently. With deep, measured thrusts, he began to probe her warm depths. With each thrust he heard her gasp in pleasure. Laughing happily, she reached up to pull him toward her, thrusting her buttocks up to meet each downward thrust.

They went at it for a while, the bed squeaking under them, beads of perspiration standing out on her shoulders and breasts until Longarm found himself mounting inexorably to his climax. Rita's arms tightened about his neck. He buried his face in her neck and drove harder. Throwing aside all restraint, he swept past the point of no return. He heard Rita's gasps, then her sharp, inarticulate cries. At one point he thought she was screaming, but paid no heed as he continued to pound down into her.

Abruptly lifting her legs, Rita entwined her ankles behind his back, enclosing Longarm's waist in a viselike grip that pulled him still deeper into her. He pushed up onto his elbows and gazed down at her face as she began flinging her head from side to side. Then she came, uttering a long, low moan that rose to a high climax, his engorged erection pulsing wildly into her tightening, gyrating muff.

Pleasantly spent, he rolled off her. She rested her head on his shoulder and kissed him lightly on the face, then the lips.

"That was very nice," she whispered.

"It did me a lot of good too," Longarm replied, grinning at her. "After today's ride, I'm surprised I had it in me. You inspired me, Rita."

"I am glad," she purred, snuggling still closer.

For a long while, Longarm lay quietly on his back beside her, aware of the warm, sweet smell of her, the gentle feel of her exhaling breath on his chest. For a moment he thought she had fallen asleep. When she stirred, he realized she was still awake.

"Rita," he said.

"Yes, Custis?"

"I'm looking for four men, two of them wounded. They would have ridden in here maybe a week back with saddlebags filled with gold dust."

She lifted her head and peered closely at him. "You are a lawman?"

He nodded. "And I want those men."

"I have seen the men you seek," she whispered.

"One of the gang's members is a man called Turco."

"I remember him. He has the face of a rat, that one."

"What else do you remember, Rita?"

She told him then of four men who had ridden into Big Rock, taken rooms in the hotel, and proceeded to

21

pay generously in gold dust for whatever they wanted. Their leader—a man called Cheyenne—played poker and faro almost around the clock, losing great amounts of gold dust without complaint. The two wounded men had remained in their rooms while the girls tended their wounds—and their other needs. From what these girls had told Rita, neither man's hungers or capacities had been lessened by their wounds. Rita had done her best to keep out of their way.

"Rita," Longarm told her when she had finished, "that gold dust Cheyenne was gambling with he and his men stole from a Wells Fargo express office in Idaho."

"Are you Pinkerton man? You work for Wells Fargo?"

"I don't work for Wells Fargo," Longarm told her, "and I'm not a Pinkerton."

"Oh . . ."

Before leaving Summit, Longarm had telegraphed Vail and told him he was going to keep after Turco and while he was at it, do what he could to overhaul the other outlaws who had robbed the Wells Fargo express office. After a wait of two days, Vail had telegraphed him to get Turco first and worry about the Cheyenne Kid later. Which was as close to a blank check as Longarm was likely to get from Billy.

"Then who are you?"

"A federal marshal. Keep that to yourself, will you, Rita?"

"I will tell no one, Custis."

"Have they pulled out?"

"Yes. Three days ago. Something bad happen. They leave after that."

"What happened?"

22

"Cheyenne gamble and drink and then he say the one who is taking his money is cheating. He draw his gun and shoot the man twice."

That sounded like Cheyenne, all right. A bored, restless man looking for an excuse to move on. Longarm had no doubt now that he would catch up to him. And he was not forgetting Len Turco either.

At the moment he was having trouble keeping his eyes open. He had been bone-tired when he climbed the stairs to his room after Rita. For a while her feminine wiles had enabled him forget how exhausted he was. But no longer was he able to fight back the fatigue that now sat like anvils on his eyelids. He smiled weakly at Rita.

"I think I am going to fall to sleep any minute," he told her. "Maybe you better get on downstairs."

"*Sí,*" she said, sitting up and smiling down at him. "I am afraid I have tire you out."

"I wasn't complaining."

"I know," she said.

She leaned close and kissed him lightly on the forehead, then pulled the covers up over his naked body. As the cool sheet fell over him, Longarm closed his eyes and dropped off into a sweet, bottomless pit.

Chapter 3

A cannon went off under Longarm's bed. Or that was how it sounded. He came awake in an instant and jumped out of bed. In the pale light of dawn he saw he was alone in his room.

From outside his room came the scuffle of footsteps, startled shouts, then the sound of a man crying out in rage and panic. Longarm snatched his .44 from under his pillow, ran to the door, and flung it open. The hallway was thick with an acrid pall of gunpowder, and standing resolutely by the door—an overturned chair behind her—was Rita, an enormous Walker Colt clutched in both hands.

Pete's dirty face stared wide-eyed at him from the stairwell a moment before he ducked below the floor level. In the wall just above his descending head was a neat hole where Rita's bullet had gone. Longarm righted Rita's overturned chair and smiled gratefully at her.

"Looks like you just kept them two from visitin' me."

She nodded weakly at him, her face chalk-white. But her jaw was set with an iron resolve. Then her eyes widened.

"Custis! You are naked!"

As footsteps pounded up the stairs, Rita pushed Longarm back into his room and closed the door behind them. Grinning sheepishly, Longarm hurried to his bed, and was pulling on his long underwear when the door burst open and Bingham rushed in.

"I heard shooting!" he cried.

"One shot," Longarm said, correcting him. "To scare off Pete. He was on his way up here to make trouble."

Bingham looked in some surprise at Rita. She was still holding the Walker Colt. "That right, Rita?"

"*Sí,*" she told him. "It is like he say."

With a weary nod, the hotel owner pulled the door shut. As soon as he was gone, Longarm finished dressing.

"Rita," he asked, "were you out there all night?"

"*Sí,*" she replied, "but I fall asleep. I am so sorry."

"Hey, you got no cause to feel bad," he told her, grinning. "From the looks of it, you did just fine."

"The board in the floor, it squeak. I open my eyes and see Pete. He is almost to the door. I am so crazy with surprise, I jump up. When he run down the stairs I pull the trigger without I aim first."

"It's a good thing you didn't aim," he told her. "You might have killed the son of a bitch. I don't think you'd like that." He glanced at the ancient firearm in her hand. "By the way, where'd you get that cannon?"

"My grandfather. When he send me up here, he pack it with my things. I did not know it would make such a loud noise. It have the kick of a bull."

"Better put it back, Rita."

"*Sí.* I will do that."

"Last night, Rita, you said Cheyenne left three days ago."

She nodded.

"Which way'd they go?"

She pointed out the window, indicating the direction they took. "I heard them mention Black Pine Gap."

"You saw them leave?"

She nodded. "Mr. Bingham and I, we bury this gambler Cheyenne kill. They see us when they ride out, but they do not stop." Rita shook her head at such lack of compassion. "You must be careful if you go after such men, Custis. They are all devils, I think."

"Devils or not, I have no choice in the matter. Promise not to tell anyone here that I'm after Cheyenne. He must have many friends left around here."

"I will tell no one," she said.

"Thanks, Rita."

"And now I must go down and help in the kitchen to prepare for the breakfast."

He watched her leave, then sat back down on his bed and reached for his boots. The flesh wound in his side, he noted with some satisfaction, was no longer bothering him.

Longarm checked out, then entered the dining room. He found an empty table and sat down, piling his saddlebags on the chair beside him. Except for the livery stable owner and one other townsman, the dining room was empty. Out from the kitchen popped Rita. A smile on her face, she hurried over to his table.

"Mr. Bingham, he say I can join you for breakfast."

Longarm pulled a chair out for her, then shoved it gently in under her as she sat down.

"Ah, Custis!" she said, smiling up at him. "You are so gallant."

"And you are very brave."

She blushed. He sat down and took her hand in his.

"You got that cannon in a safe place?"

"Oh, yes. I put it under my pillow."

He laughed. "Maybe around here that's not such a bad idea. But just take care you don't blow your head off. Be sure the hammer is not resting on a loaded cylinder."

"Yes, Custis. My grandfather, he show me."

One of the bar girls, transformed overnight into a waitress, came over to take their order. Before she did, she winked at Rita. As she hurried off a moment later, Bingham entered the dining room, caught sight of them, and hurried over to their table.

"Are you all right, Rita?" he asked.

"Yes, *Señor* Bingham. I am fine."

"And you, Mr. Long?"

"I'm fine. Thanks to Rita—and that cannon of hers."

"Ah, yes," the owner said, smiling at Rita. "That famous Walker Colt."

"Sit down, Bingham," Longarm said.

"My friends call me Bing," the little round man said as he pulled up a chair.

"Bing," said Longarm, "I don't want any reprisals for what Rita did outside my door this morning. It don't look like there's any law in this town, so she more than likely saved my life." He dug out two double eagles from his side pocket of his jacket and handed them to the hotel owner. "There's a bullet hole in the wall upstairs. That should take care of the damage."

Bingham's eyes went wide. "This is more than enough, Mr. Long. Thank you. Rita's a good girl. I didn't want her to go up with those two animals. She is not like the other girls." As he spoke, he reached over and patted Rita on the arm.

"Where are those two now?"

"They rode out after Rita took that shot at Pete."

"Good riddance," said Rita, her voice hushed with relief.

When Longarm and Rita's orders arrived, Bingham excused himself and left the dining room. Longarm found that breakfast with Rita was a delight. Her banter was light, and more than once she had Longarm laughing out loud. There was more—much more—to this young Mexican girl than Longarm would have guessed.

Their breakfast done, Longarm pushed away his plate and finished his second cup of coffee.

"Are you going now?" Rita asked.

Longarm nodded.

"Your wound. Is it better?"

"I hardly know it's there."

Impulsively, Rita took Longarm's face in her hands and pulled him close so she could kiss him. It was a long, passionate, good-bye kiss; and when it was done, she turned and darted from the dining room. Longarm watched her go, aware of a sharp sense of loss. He took a deep breath, gathered up his gear, and strode from the hotel.

Four days later on the other side of Black Pine Gap, Longarm rode out onto a ledge and looked down at a scruffy-looking nest of ranch buildings shaded by cottonwoods. The ranch appeared to be deserted. The pole corral behind the horse barn was empty, and for as long as he sat his horse watching, not a single ranch hand moved between the buildings. No smoke curled out of the lodgepole cabin's chimney. For a while longer Longarm sat his horse, then pulled the black off the ledge and started down the narrow trail that led to the valley floor.

Not long after, Longarm splashed through a shallow stream and rode into the cottonwoods shading the spread. Pulling up, he again sat his black awhile as he surveyed the silent ranch house. From somewhere in the branches above him came the hard chattering of a chipmunk. Chickens clucked about in the thick grass around a small shed behind the ranch house. He rode closer to the cabin and saw a small covey of bobwhites feeding on a patch of clover near the chimney, which meant— at least for now—the cabin was deserted. He rode across the compound to the hitch rail, called a hello to the cabin without expecting any response, got none, dismounted, and entered. The large kitchen and living room was a mess. The place had been poorly used. Broken crockery littered one side of the room, the rough, wooden china cabinet that had held the crockery resting on top of the wreckage. Partially consumed pieces of a chair were lying in the fireplace, and a greasy pile of dishes sat in a wooden bucket in the sink, the shelves over it cleaned out, stripped of anything of value to men on the trail. There was no mystery what had happened here.

Cheyenne and his gang had been here before him.

The sound of the bobwhites exploding in sudden panic caused Longarm to turn. A hulking shadow loomed in the doorway, a shotgun in his hand. Longarm dodged to one side and flung himself to the floor an instant before the shotgun's boom filled the cabin's interior. The buckshot went wild, and before the man in the doorway could fire again, Longarm hit him low and drove him back out through the doorway, the shotgun discharging its second barrel into the air. Before Longarm's driving charge, the man folded back with surprisingly little resistance. As the man staggered unsteadily, Longarm drew his .44 and clubbed him on the side of the head. The man lost all fight instantly and collapsed to the ground, coming to rest faceup. Only then did Longarm notice the matted blood covering his left shoulder.

"Don't shoot!" the downed man cried feebly.

"Why the hell not? You just tried to cut me in half with that shotgun."

"You was in my place. Besides . . . I thought you was one of them . . . come back."

"Cheyenne's gang?"

"Yeah. They camped out here. Took my food—and my woman. Who the hell are you?"

Longarm told him, then asked the rancher's name.

"Jack Collins."

"Can you get up?"

"That was a mean crack you gave me," he snarled.

31

"And I've lost a lot of blood from this shoulder wound."

"Well, I'm not going to carry you into that cabin. You'll have to make it on your own."

"All right. All right. I can make it."

Slowly, painfully, Collins pushed himself upright, then tottered into the cabin and slumped into a chair at the kitchen table. Lugging the shotgun, Longarm followed him in and leaned the weapon in a corner near the fireplace. Then he took a good look at his would-be assailant. Collins was in his early forties, his hair graying. There was a softness about his mouth and an evasiveness in his eyes that told Longarm that Collins was the kind who took the easy road whenever it was offered, a man always hoping for the break that never came as he sank deeper into shit.

"I'm wounded bad," Collins complained. "You got to help me."

Longarm walked over to Collins and looked more closely at his shoulder wound. The area around it looked ugly enough, but the entry wound was scabbing over quickly. Collins had probably lost considerable blood, but the bullet had gone clean through without shattering the collarbone, and with the wound closing up, he did not appear to be in any danger.

"When did you take this slug?" Longarm asked.

"This morning. At the creek. I was chasing after them."

"Because they stole your woman?"

"Yeah, that's right. That's what I said, ain't it?"

"It looks like you'll live," Longarm said, stepping back. "All you got's a flesh wound."

"I can hardly move my arm."

"But you *can* move it."

"Some."

"Rest easy and I'll see what I can rustle up."

"There's some beans under the sink them bastards missed," Collins told him.

Collins pushed himself upright and tottered into his bedroom. Longarm went outside to see to the black, then returned to the cabin and found the cans of beans under the sink as well as a jug of tequila. It had plenty of punch and went well with the beans Longarm cooked in a cast-iron pot on the wood stove. He brought a generous portion of beans in to Collins on a partially shattered platter along with a tin cup of tequila. But Collins was so exhausted Longarm could not arouse him. With a shrug, he finished the beans himself, drank the cup of tequila, and left the house, preferring to spend the night under the stars.

The next morning he returned to the cabin and found Collins trying to get a fire going in the wood stove. He was cursing a lot and getting nowhere. The jug of tequila was sitting, uncorked, on the table. Longarm nudged him aside, spied some embers gleaming in the bottom of the firebox, and soon had a fire going. Collins stepped back, making no effort to help or pick up any of the litter Cheyenne's gang had left. When he saw Longarm had things under control, he sat down at the table; sucking occasionally on the jug of tequila, he watched without comment as Longarm brewed the coffee and warmed two more cans of beans.

After they finished breakfast, Longarm asked Collins which way the Cheyenne Kid had gone.

"Through White Horn Pass. Looks like they're

headin' for Montana Territory."

"They're a full day's ride ahead of me then."

"No, they ain't."

"How so?"

"You can overtake them easy by goin' through the mountain and meetin' them on the other side of the pass. Just follow the river into the canyon. You'll come to a waterfall and see a trail goes up the canyon wall. Follow that."

"Follow the river?"

"I mean keep in the riverbed. It's the only way. You could never make it following the riverbank. The water's still fast, but you can make it. There's no other way through the mountains."

Longarm stood up. "I'll be ridin' out now then. You goin' to be all right?"

"I'll be fine. You just get after them. I want my Rose back. I'd go with you, but they took all my horseflesh."

"I'll do what I can, Collins."

"Just get them bastards."

Collins lifted the jug to his lips and gulped down a hefty swig. Longarm glanced around him at the ruined cabin. It was a depressing sight. He knew there were only six more cans of beans left, and he could not help wondering how long this poor son of a bitch would last when they were gone—and he'd flung the last of that tequila down his gullet.

"I'll do what I can," Longarm told him.

"Tell Rose I'll take her back. It don't matter what them men made her do."

Longarm turned and walked out of the cabin.

● ● ●

He reached the canyon two hours later, then put the black into the swift water and started upstream. In places the stream reached a depth of at least four feet, and soon his thighs were soaked and his boots heavy with moisture. On both sides of him, sheer walls of rock soared skyward, cutting off the sunlight almost completely.

The black stumbled occasionally as its hooves struggled forward over the riverbed's smooth gravel. Longarm patted its neck and soothed it with soft words of encouragement—and kept on. Collins had been right about the impossibility of riding along the shoreline. A mountain goat would have had difficulty following it. Longarm could imagine how high this stream must rise during the spring runoff. There would be no shoreline at all.

The water's force increased as the slope of the streambed lifted. Each time Longarm glanced up at the bright slash of blue sky overhead, it seemed to have receded still farther from him. After a while he came to an abrupt turn and found himself approaching a stretch of white water. The black snorted nervously and shook its head emphatically as if it was not at all happy at the prospect of continuing on, but Longarm would not let it pause.

About a mile further into the canyon, he put the rapids behind him, and the water became so smooth and clear that when he glanced down at the streambed, it was as if he were looking through a pane of glass. The pines clinging to the sheer rock walls were smaller now, the great, perpendicular slabs of rock through which the stream had cut its way appeared to be leaning still closer, and the strip of blue sky was no longer visible. It was as if he had ridden into a wet subterranean world. He soon became aware of a distant roaring—like the murmur of wind in the tops of pines. A moment later the black carried him around a shoulder of rock and he saw a column of mist rising from the streambed ahead of him. He kept on, and before long a light mantle of spray began falling onto him.

This was the waterfall Collins had mentioned.

About fifty yards further on, at the edge of a deep pool, he glanced up and saw a thin plume of water plunging toward him at such a height that by the time it was three quarters of the way down, it had become as delicate as a lace curtain. He looked away and caught sight of the game trail Collins had mentioned leading to the canyon's rim. He put his black out of the stream, rode over to the trail, and started up it.

The trail's short switchback loops took Longarm steadily higher until the stream he had left behind was no longer visible and the sound of the waterfall only a whisper hanging in the air. Sometime past noon he saw the entrance to what appeared to be an abandoned mine, dismounted, and made his noon camp. To one side of the mine's entrance, there was a thin stream and a small patch of grass. There he filled his canteen and picketed the black. He dined on sourdough biscuits and jerky, then mounted up and continued on up the winding trail.

He was soon so high he felt the effects of a chill wind blowing off the snow-clad peaks surrounding him. He kept going past sunset. Before long he was riding through a night as black as pitch. The trail was too narrow for him to make camp, so he kept going. He

36

felt the trail dropping slightly, and realized he had passed the canyon's rim and was heading for the floor of the pass below. He kept on despite the fact that the trail appeared to be narrowing. Before long, he was forced to keep the black so close to the cliff face his trousers brushed the rock.

Close to the end of its string by this time, the black pulled up frequently, going on only after Longarm's insistent boot heels urged him to do so. At one spot the trail pitched so steeply downward that the black's hooves slid forward over the loose gravel for a couple of yards before he was able to regain solid footing.

Longarm had descended at least a hundred feet when the black refused to move on. No matter how hard he strained to see ahead of him, Longarm could pick out no shape—nothing but an awesome, yawning emptiness. Then he thought he could make out the dim tracery of the trail extending ahead of him along, close along the cliff side. He applied his spurs gently to the black's flanks. But the horse would have none of it. At last Longarm gave up and leaned back in his saddle.

"All right, horse," he muttered. "Which way is it?"

The black shook its head, then gathered its feet close together and began to wind slowly about in small shifts until it had turned competely around. Only then, once more on its way down, did it move on. Longarm glanced back, and in that instant saw the spot where the trail had switched back, realizing he had missed it in the stygian gloom. Had he insisted on proceeding straight on, he would have launched himself and the black into space. Longarm patted the black's neck gratefully and, leaning back in the saddle, he let the reins go slack.

His progress became much slower from then on. But the black kept on steadily, and soon Longarm could hear the echo of their passage coming from solid ground below him. The trail reached level ground at last, the clash of the horse's shod hooves echoing off rock walls on either side of him. Glancing up, he made out a small, faint wedge of stars. He took off his hat, wiped his brow with the back of his forearm, slapped the hat back on, and dug his heels into the black's flank. A moment later, he felt as well as saw the night sky open out before him and glancing up, saw a swarm of stars, then a bright orange peel of a moon swim into view.

He was exhausted, and the stumbling feel of the black under him communicated the same distress. He came on a stream coursing close under a ponderous shoulder of rock. Dismounting, he unsaddled the black, then hobbled it, letting it find its own graze. Too weary to bother with a campfire or anything to eat, Longarm slumped down onto a grassy patch, his head resting back against his saddle, and pulled his slicker around him. Before he closed his eyes, he told himself not to sleep beyond daybreak.

Sleep came instantly—like a gentle fist.

Chapter 4

Longarm awoke quickly, aware at once of the gray light,
unhappy that he had slept past dawn. Shivering, he sat up
and rubbed his hands together. His slicker was dimpled
with beads of dew, and he could see his breath. He got
up and stretched, the chill morning breeze buffeting him.
Though it was only September, at this height there was
already a hint of frost in the air.

He poked with his rifle barrel under the edges of
boulders for snakes, then gathered firewood and built a
fire. He sat his spider pan atop the flames, then fried his
remaining sourdough biscuits in bacon fat along with the
last of his jerky. He was reaching for the coffeepot when
he saw the black raise its head in sudden alarm and take
a step backward. Behind him, Longarm heard the chink
of spurs.

He drew his Colt and spun around—to find himself
staring into the bore of a six-gun. The one holding it
was Pete, the raw-faced gent he had handled none too

gently in the Big Rock hotel. His partner, Rick, stood beside him, showing his broken teeth in a yellow smile, his own Colt drawn.

"Drop the iron, you big ugly son of a bitch," Pete said.

Longarm dropped his Colt. Pete grinned wickedly, took a quick step forward, and smashed Longarm across the side of the face with the barrel of his revolver. The blow was carefully measured and Pete put all the force he could muster into it. Longarm spun to the ground, the back of his head crunching against a boulder. Doing his best to shake off its effects, he glared up at the two men. Rick thrust his foxlike snout close to Longarm's.

"We seen you at the Collins place. Cheyenne told us he'd kilt him, so we was thinkin' of taking the ranch over. But we saw Collins. He didn't look dead to us. He ain't dead, is he?"

"He's wounded, that's all."

"Shit," said Rick, glancing unhappily at his partner.

"It was Collins told you, wasn't it?" said Pete.

"Told me what?"

"Where our mine was. We seen you ride by later. You was pretty smart about it. You just rested a while, then kept on. You acted like you didn't even want to look inside it. But that didn't fool us."

"You're crazy. Collins told me nothing about your mine."

"Then how'd you find that trail?" Pete demanded.

"Collins."

"See? You ain't very smart, mister, tryin' to fool us."

"Collins was just giving me a way to get through the pass quicker. He didn't mention anything about your mine."

"So how come you're so anxious to get to this pass?"

"That's my business."

"No, it ain't," Pete told him. "It's our business now."

Rick moved closer and went swiftly through Longarm's pockets. Out of the inside pocket in Longarm's frock coat he pulled a wallet, and opened it to reveal the silver federal badge pinned to it.

"What the hell! You a lawman?"

"You saw the badge."

"This's a federal badge. Who're you after?"

"Hell," Pete said, "that ain't no mystery. He's after the Cheyenne Kid. For that Wells Fargo heist in Idaho."

"That right, mister? You after the Kid?"

Longarm nodded.

"Well, well, well. If that ain't just dandy," Rick said, his yellowish eyes alight. He glanced at Pete. "Why don't we do Cheyenne a favor?"

"What do you mean?"

"I say we present this lawman to Cheyenne, all hog-tied and ready for hanging."

"You're right. He'd sure be grateful to get this lawman off his back."

"Yeah," Rick said. "Grateful enough to maybe open up some of them gold dust bags."

"His saddlebags are jammed full with gold dust," Pete said, eyes wide with greed. "I watched him packing his gear when he pulled out of Big Rock. No reason why he shouldn't be generous if we do him a real favor."

41

Both men turned to gaze at Longarm as if he were a winning sweepstakes ticket and Cheyenne was about to redeem it, which meant these two must know where the outlaw was camped. Longarm leaned wearily back against the boulder. It looked like he was going to catch up to Cheyenne a lot sooner than he had expected.

The man Longarm assumed was Cheyenne was squatting by the morning fire, pouring himself a cup of coffee, when Longarm rode into his camp ahead of his two captors, a noose looped over his neck. The Kid stood up and flung his coffee away. The others in his camp got to their feet also. Some distance back, standing between two men, Longarm saw a woman he figured was Jack Collins's wife.

An annoyed frown on his face, Cheyenne waited for them to reach him. He was tall with a dark olive complexion, blazing dark eyes, and eyebrows that canted upward, giving him a faintly saturnine cast. For a notorious outlaw forever on the dodge, he was dressed cleanly and well with a black leather vest and tight-fitting calfskin britches. The sweatband of his black sombrero was decorated with silver conchos.

Pulling his black to a halt, Longarm met Cheyenne's gaze without saying a word. Cheyenne looked past Longarm at Pete and Rick.

"What the hell are you two up to?" he demanded. "Who's this guy?"

"He's a present we got for you," Rick crowed.

"Speak plain, dammit!"

"Meet Custis Long, a U. S. marshal," said Pete. "He's trackin' you for some reason. Maybe that heist in Idaho."

His dark brows canting, the Kid looked back at Longarm. "That right?"

Longarm nodded.

"You mean you come after me all the way from Idaho?"

"That's right, Cheyenne."

"Why?"

"Sam Calder is dead."

"Jesus," Cheyenne said. "I didn't mean for that to happen. I must've shot too fast. I aimed for Sam's leg. I just wanted to disable him—not kill him."

"You're a lousy shot, Cheyenne. That bullet of yours tore up his gut."

Cheyenne's face seemed to cave in. Then he stepped back. Addressing Pete and Rick, he said, "Light and set a spell. We still got coffee. Help yourself."

"Hey, Kid," Pete said, "you goin' to take this lawman off our hands?"

"I'm thinkin' on it."

Pete dismounted, the rope looped over Longarm's head still held in his hands. Without warning, he yanked on the rope. Longarm toppled from the horse and landed heavily. He snapped the noose off his neck and leaped to his feet. Pete and Rick, grins on their faces, their guns drawn, waited for Longarm to charge them.

"Go get your coffee," the Kid told them.

"Don't you want us to soften him up a little?" asked Pete.

"No. I want you two vultures to drink your coffee, then get the hell out of here."

"You mean you ain't grateful we brung him to you?"

"Okay. Okay. I'm grateful."

"Well, then, we figured with all that gold dust maybe you could maybe part with a little of it."

"In gratitude," said Rick, "sort of."

Cheyenne looked at the two men as if he had just overturned a rock. "I ain't givin' you two vultures nothin'. Except that coffee. You want it? If you don't, ride out."

Properly chastened, the two scurried over to the fire.

"You had breakfast yet?" the Kid asked Longarm.

"No."

"Stay here and don't try anything. I'll have Rose bring over some grub."

As the Kid moved off, Longarm slumped down onto the ground, resting his back against a small pine. He was not unduly weary, since his camp had been no more than a mile from Cheyenne's campsite. He was not entirely dispirited. Pete and Rick had not discovered the derringer in his vest pocket, and during the ride, he had managed to tuck the belly gun down into the back of his right boot. The low-heeled cavalry stovepipes he preferred did not allow much room for the weapon, and there was a slight bulge visible to anyone smart enough to look for it. But so far no one had been that smart.

The Kid was conferring with his three gang members, no doubt considering the quickest way to dispose of a federal lawman. Rose Collins came over with a tin plate piled with beans and jerky, a cup of steaming black coffee perched on the side of the plate.

She said nothing to him, simply standing over him as he sipped his coffee and cleaned off the plate. She was dressed in a man's shirt and Levi's, filling them out as no man could. A yellow scarf was knotted at her neck, and her dark hair, thick and curly, hung down to her shoulders. Her face was narrow, with sharp, angular lines. She was not very pretty, but there was a feral look in her smoky eyes that could excite a man—and keep him turned on.

Longarm handed up the tin plate and cup to her.

"Rose, your husband is worried about you."

She was startled. "You know Jack?"

Longarm nodded.

"He sent you after me?"

"He said he loves you and wants you back. He said it doesn't matter to him what these men made you do. He'll take you back."

She laughed, shortly, contemptuously. "Take me back, will he? That fool! I swear, he'd eat my vomit if I told him to. Go back to him? I'd rather die!"

"Then you didn't leave him against your will?"

"Mister, I would have gone off with the devil himself if he had asked me. Jack Collins is a loser. And a whiner. He has the backbone of a jellyfish. I was such a fool to have married him. I should have stayed in Big Rock at Bingham's."

Longarm had suspected as much from the beginning.

"Don't worry," he told her. "I'll make no effort to take you back."

"Don't look like I'll have to worry about that. You ain't goin' to take anyone back—and that includes yourself, I'm thinking."

He watched Rose head back to the camp fire, wondering at all the men whose wives loathed them—and all the women who bored their husbands silly. It was a losing situation. Sometimes, the more a man loved his woman, the greater the contempt she felt for him; and if a woman was obedient and loyal to her man, the more restless and unfaithful he became.

Longarm studied Cheyenne's three gang members. Len Turco, with his receding chin and wild eyes, stood out like a tarantula on a wedding cake. The outlaw next to him—a tall, lanky fellow—still had his arm in a sling. The third outlaw was a monstrously fat buffalo of a man who seemed to have recovered completely. For a while Longarm wondered if these two were aware that he had been the one firing at them from the shop window as they galloped out of Summit, then decided that they had been so busy shagging ass, they hadn't had the time to get a good look at him.

Abruptly Cheyenne left his men and walked over to Pete and Rick. The two miners were hunkered around the fire, but stood up quickly as Cheyenne approached. Longarm could see the naked hope in their expressions. Now they were going to get their reward for bringing Longarm in. Cheyenne spoke to them in a low voice, curtly, sharply. Immediately the two men were outraged. In their fury, they clawed for their six-guns, but Cheyenne's draw was so far ahead of them, both men were covered before their six-guns cleared leather. The Kid waved his men over.

"Disarm these two cockroaches," he told them loudly. "Then break camp and dump their gear about a half mile further on. After that, keep going. I'll catch up."

The three were more than thorough as they relieved the miners of their six-guns, a couple of knives, and a rifle. Then, with Rose's help, they began breaking camp. Cheyenne started for Longarm. As he approached, Longarm considered going for the derringer tucked in his boot, but he had just witnessed Cheyenne's prowess with a six-gun, and besides, there were only two rounds in the derringer.

Cheyenne hunkered down beside Longarm, took out a cheroot, lit it, then offered one to Longarm. Longarm took it without a word, bit off the end, then leaned close as Cheyenne lit it for him.

"That's a nice black you got there," Cheyenne said.

Longarm inhaled deeply, exhaling through his nostrils, the bite of the tobacco a real pleasure under the circumstances.

"Yeah. It's a fine horse."

"I'll leave it down the road a ways, saddled and carrying your .44, your Winchester, and the rest of your gear—just in case."

Longarm had no idea what Cheyenne was up to, but said nothing and took a deep drag on the cheroot. The three outlaws, with Rose helping, finished breaking camp and mounted up. Hazing the miners' horses ahead of them, they rode out. Longarm went back to his cheroot, waiting for Cheyenne to make his intentions clear. Cheyenne cleared his throat.

"I got to kill you, mister."

"My name's Long. Custis Long."

"Yeah. I know. Sam used to talk a good deal about you."

"He was a good friend, a man you could count on."

"I know that."

Longarm took a drag on his cheroot.

47

"Thing is, after what happened, I feel like maybe I owe you something."

"You don't owe me anything."

The Kid frowned intently as he gazed off into the distance. "A tinhorn marshal left me with a bullet in my gut, near dead by a water hole. I only had a few feet to go, but there was no way in hell I was going to make it to that water. Calder rode up, gave me water, then fished the slug out of me. He tended me like a brother till I got back on my feet."

The Kid went silent then, pulling on the cheroot, his eyes narrow slits peering at the coiling wreaths of smoke.

"Afterward we rode together," he resumed, his voice still soft, "and pulled a few jobs. But Sam didn't like that much. He was always thinking of the poor sons of bitches we was robbin'. He didn't have the heart for it. So he went his way, and I went mine—no hard feelings. You got to believe me, Long. When Sam walked into that express office, I was so surprised, I just wasn't thinkin' clear."

"You thought clear enough to kill him."

"I told you! I didn't mean that."

Longarm said nothing.

"No more talk," the Kid said bleakly. "Because you was his friend, I'm giving you a chance. And that's all it is. A chance. I'm leaving you here with these two vermin. I promised them plenty of gold dust if they kill you."

"Thanks."

"Hear me out, Long. I told them they had to use their bare hands, and bring me your wallet as proof they'd finished you off. Otherwise, no gold dust."

Without a word, Longarm looked at the man.

"It's the best I can do for you."

Leaning close, the Kid tucked Longarm's wallet into his inside coat pocket, then flipped aside the frock coat, and was reaching for the watch fob pocket in Longarm's vest when he saw the gold chain hanging loose. He smiled coldly at Longarm.

"Okay. Where is it?"

"Where's what?"

"The belly gun sits in that watch-fob pocket. Sam told me about that cheater too. One of your trademarks."

"I lost it."

"Bullshit."

Cheyenne stood up and surveyed Longarm critically. When his eyes focused on Longarm's boots, they lit suddenly. He bent quickly and slipped the derringer out of the boot, then dropped it into his side pocket.

"I'll tuck this into your bedroll," he promised.

"See that you do, Cheyenne. I'll be needin' it."

"That's the spirit," he said.

He left Longarm and strode over to his horse. As he passed the two miners, he barked something at them, then stepped into his saddle and without a glance back spurred off down the trail. As the drumbeat of his horse's hooves faded, the two miners, licking their lips nervously, started toward Longarm. A few yards from Longarm, Pete bent and picked up a fist-sized rock. His partner did the same. Longarm got to his feet, flipped the cheroot at the two men, then moved cautiously away from the boulder to give himself more room.

Rick hurled his rock at Longarm's head, then charged. Longarm ducked. The rock sailed past his shoulder, and a second later Rick plowed into him, driving him back against the boulder. Lights exploded deep inside his skull, and before he could break free of Rick, Pete hit him from the side, using the rock in his hand to hammer Longarm's head. He heard his shirt rip as he twisted wildly and managed to knock the rock out of Pete's grasp; but Rick hooked an arm around his neck, and the two of them—clawing wildly at him—attempted to force him to the ground.

Under the weight of their furious assault, Longarm sagged to one knee, steadied himself, and then jabbed back savagely with his elbow, breaking Pete's grip. With his left fist he lashed out and caught Rick in his Adam's apple. Uttering a strangled cry, Rick staggered back, both hands clutching at his throat. Surging up onto his feet, Longarm turned his full attention on Pete, slashing at his face and head. As Pete sagged forward under Longarm's fierce battering, Longarm brought up his knee and slammed it into Pete's face, exploding his nose.

From behind, Rick threw himself onto Longarm, pummeling him with a wild flurry of blows. Longarm swung about to fight him off. The tip of an embedded boulder caught his boot. He stumbled and went down. Instantly, both men were on top of him, pounding him with their fists. He could feel himself losing his bearings and covered his head with his forearms, then heaved desperately to one side and managed to roll out of their grasp, then pushed himself up onto his hands and knees. His right hand found a loose rock. He spun about and flung it into Rick's face. The rock crunched into the man's cheekbone. He spun away, yelping like a whipped cur.

As Pete rushed him, Longarm kicked him in the mouth. The man staggered backward, spitting out teeth. His heel caught a boulder and he went down heavily on his back—just as Rick, raving like a madman, rammed his head into Longarm's back and drove him forward to the ground. Longarm hit heavily and lay there, dazed for a moment, then instinctively flung himself over onto his back.

Rick, his face distorted with madness, stood over him, a huge rock held high over his head. Longarm flung himself aside just as Rick flung the boulder down at him. It crunched into the ground, missing him by inches. Longarm scrambled to his feet in time to sidestep Rick's charge, then bent to pick up a fist-sized rock. Before he could use it on Rick, Pete grabbed him from behind and yanked him around. Grappling frantically, the two men thudded heavily to the ground. But Longarm still held the rock. Using it like a club, he drove it viciously against Pete's head. Again and again he struck Pete's skull until he felt it give way. Pete sagged forward. His body shuddered convulsively, then lay still.

Uttering a wild, inchoate scream, Rick flung himself onto Longarm, a long sliver of rock in his hands. Wielding it like a knife, he slashed clumsily at Longarm's face and head, managing only a few glancing blows. Grasping Rick's wrist with both hands, Longarm twisted. Rick's wrist snapped and he dropped his crude weapon. Longarm stood up and yanked Rick upright after him.

A wild blood lust fired Longarm now, banishing all fatigue, as he punched Rick with savage, murderous precision. Slowly Rick backed up under the furious onslaught, unable to do much more than paw feebly at Longarm. Blood streamed from his shattered nose and mouth, and he began to whimper like a child. Finally—in a desperate, mindless attempt to escape his tormentor— he put his head down and lunged blindly at Longarm.

As Rick struck him, Longarm brought the edge of his palm down on the back of his neck, dropping Rick like a poleaxed steer. He hit the ground with a heavy crunch—and moved not an inch further. A spreading slick of blood oozed out from under his face. Longarm bent over, grabbed his shoulder, and rolled him over. Rick's face had come down on a sharply ridged stone embedded in the ground, which had shattered the bone between his eyes and thrust its shards deep into Rick's brain.

He was dead. And so was Pete. It was over.

Longarm turned Rick back over onto his stomach, and for the first time became aware of the ugly, rasping sound he was making as he sucked air into his heaving lungs. He sounded like a wild animal. A sudden giddiness overtook him and in order to stay upright, he was forced to spread his feet like a sailor on a heaving deck. The dizziness passed, his labored breathing quieted, and he slumped wearily to the ground to inspect his ragged clothes. One knee was out in his trousers and his shirt was ripped in at least three places. His frock coat's left pocket was ripped clean off, and his vest had been torn nearly in half. He glanced skyward and saw two buzzards drifting lazily overhead. There would be more soon. He pushed himself upright, retrieved his hat, and did his best to dust it off. Then he clapped it on his head and started down the trail.

Cheyenne had promised he would leave Longarm's black and his gear further down the trail, and Longarm hoped sincerely the outlaw had not been lying. Longarm had some spare clothes with his gear. They weren't fancy, but they'd do. A moment later when he rounded a bend in the trail and saw his saddled black cropping the grass alongside the trail, he decided he owed Cheyenne.

But not all that much.

Chapter 5

Longarm crested a ridge and rode along its spine until he came in sight of the town. He was not unfamiliar with this country, and had passed through the town a few years back. He pulled up and thumbed back his Stetson. Below him the dim trace he had been following disappeared into the thick stand of lodgepole pine clothing the steep foothill. Beyond the timber the gleam of a broad stream was visible as it meandered across the valley floor; it was alongside this stream that the town had been planted. He caught the glint of the late afternoon sun as it flashed off windows. After a week on Cheyenne's trail this gleam was a welcome sight.

He urged his horse on down the trace, and an hour before sundown rode in. A wooden sign riddled with bullets said WELCOME TO GALLSTONE. As he rode down Gallstone's main street he kept alert for a tailor shop, and at length spotted WONG'S TAILOR SHOPPE squeezed between the barbershop and the saddlery. He nudged his black into the hitch rack in front of it, dismounted, gathered up his torn suit and shirt from his bedroll, and entered the shop.

A smiling Mr. Wong left his steam press to wait on him. Longarm spread his torn clothing out over the counter and told the tailor what he wanted. Mr. Wong made a quick inspection of the torn trousers, frock coat, and shirt and indicated he was willing to repair them. But when it came to Longarm's vest, he shook his head.

"You got a tweed vest I can buy?" Longarm asked.

"Oh, yes. I have velly nice vest, you see."

"Show me."

Mr. Wong disappeared for a moment behind his clothing racks and returned with a hanger draped with at least a dozen vests. Longarm selected one, told the tailor he would have to make the watch-fob pocket larger, and showed him precisely how large. Mr. Wong agreed to the alteration.

"I'll be back tomorrow."

"No, solly. Too soon."

"Tomorrow morning, first thing. Chop-chop."

Mr. Wong sighed, then agreed.

Longarm left the shop, led his horse into the livery stable, and a few minutes later, his bedroll and saddlebags draped over his shoulder, kept on down the street to the Gallstone Hotel. As he mounted its veranda steps, Sheriff Ham Farnum, a bearded mountain of a man, stepped out onto the veranda—and came to an abrupt halt.

"That you, Longarm?"

"It is, Farnum."

The two men shook hands.

"You ain't aged much. Hell, you might even be getting

taller. What're you doing here? This is a long way from Denver."

"I'll explain later. Will you be in your office in a little while?"

"Maybe."

"After I check in here I'd like to talk to you."

"Come ahead."

Longarm kept on into the hotel, signed the register, and went up the stairs to his second-floor room. He checked the bed for graybacks, pulled the chamber pot out of the commode to make sure it was clean, then dumped his gear in a corner and left the hotel. When he strode into the sheriff's office, Farnum was waiting for him behind his desk, a whiskey bottle sitting on the blotter in front of him. There was only one shot glass planted beside it. Farnum always was a cheapskate. His beard was shaded from dark brown to rusty red, and from under bushy brows two gleaming, coal-black eyes peered at Longarm as they took in the scuffed Levi's and cotton shirt Longarm was wearing.

"You ain't dressed so fancy for a federal marshal."

"That's a fact," Longarm drawled, slumping into the wooden chair beside Farnum's desk. "You're getting real observant, Ham."

"Who're you after?"

"The Cheyenne Kid—and the dogs at his heels. Are they in town?"

"They are, and so far Cheyenne's keeping his tail down."

"He's wanted for the Wells Fargo Express robbery in Summit, Idaho."

"Shit, that's way out of my jurisdiction. This here's Montana Territory."

"I have a federal warrant for one of his men. Len Turco. He blew up a baggage car on the Rio Grande Western."

"That so?"

"In the course of the attempted robbery, he killed a postal employee and a federal marshal."

"Yep. Sounds like an outlaw, sure enough." Farnum poured himself some whiskey and peered with undisguised hostility at Longarm. "Seems to me, you and me tangled on a like matter once before."

"I remember. And you came out on the short end of it."

"I did and it still galls me. You won't be getting away with anything like that this time."

"All I did was take back the man I came after."

"He was in my jail in my county, and I wanted to see that murderin' son of a bitch hang."

"Don't worry. He did."

"It would have been a lot simpler if you'd let me do it."

"It would have been, I admit. But at the time it looked to me like your jail couldn't hold him."

"I don't give a whore's tit how it looked to you."

"Forget about it, Farnum. It happened so long ago, I'd forgotten all about it."

"Well, I didn't."

"That mean you won't help me take Cheyenne?"

"You can do what you want with him. And the men he rode in with. Be my guest."

"I'd appreciate your help."

"You sayin' the mighty Longarm needs Ham Farnum's help?"

"You want to crow, go ahead. But I'm still askin' for you to give me a hand."

Farnum threw the whiskey down his gullet. "I'll make it plain. I ain't gettin' involved. I like Cheyenne. He's been a good citizen while he's been here." He grinned slyly. "Not only that, but he's been very generous. A lot of merchants in town are real happy him and his boys rode in."

"That gold dust he's spreading around belongs to Wells Fargo."

Farnum shrugged. "You got the warrant, you take him."

"You won't get in my way?"

"I won't. But maybe Cheyenne will."

Longarm stood up and swept his hat off the desk. "Tell me, Ham. How much is Cheyenne paying you?"

"A damn sight more than you would—or the skinflint citizens of this here county." Ham grinned then. "Too bad you can't get your wet finger in there with the rest of us."

"Make sure your wet finger don't get chopped off."

"Trust me, Longarm. I'll be real careful."

Longarm clapped his hat on and left the office.

Longarm met Rose in the hotel lobby. She was no longer wearing a man's shirt and Levi's. But the dress she wore was cheap and frilly, and he could tell she had little on under it. She was startled to see him, perhaps even glad. He did not like the way she looked. There was a purpling bruise over her right cheekbone.

"I know," she said bitterly, her hand flying up to her cheek. "I look like hell."

"No, you don't."

"Don't be kind."

"Who did it?"

"Not Cheyenne. One of his men. Miles Pike."

"Which one is he?"

"The big fat one."

"I suggest you stay away from him."

"Tex's already taken care of that. Does Cheyenne know you're in town?"

"He will soon enough. I just came from the sheriff's office."

"You're a cool one."

"And right now I'm tired. See you, Rose."

"If you get lonely, I'll be across the street. In the Drovers Hall. Cheyenne and the house gambler have been into a high stakes poker game since four this afternoon. The Kid is certain the house gambler is cheating. Maybe you ought to go over and watch the action."

Longarm shook his head wearily. Cheyenne obviously wasn't going anywhere in a hurry, not with the town merchants and the sheriff on his side and him safe in Montana Territory. He touched the tip of his hat to Rose, moved past her, and mounted the stairs to his room. It was already dark, and as soon as he closed the door and locked it, he propped the back of a wooden chair under its doorknob. Then he pulled down the window shade and slacked back onto the bed and kicked off his boots.

Almost as soon as he stretched out, he slept.

• • •

He came awake well past midnight, aware of a growing commotion in the street below his window. He got up, pushed aside the shade, and looked down. An excited crowd was milling in front of the Drovers Hall. From the look of it, that high-stakes poker game Rose had mentioned was nearing a climax. Fully awake by now—and his mouth as dry as a gopher hole—Longarm decided it might be a good time for him to tickle his tonsils. He dressed quickly and left the hotel.

Despite the hour—it was close to two—it looked as if Gallstone's entire male population had crowded into the Drovers Hall. Longarm eased through the packed bodies, his height intimidating enough to clear a way. All he could get was a warm beer at the bar. He pulled it to him, then turned around and leaned back against the bar—and found himself standing beside the sheriff. He nodded curtly to Farnum and turned his attention to the poker game.

Cheyenne, his back to Longarm, sat facing the house gambler, two of his own men flanking him. They had discarded their cards and were now only observers. The house gambler was a cadaverous man with a blade for a nose and a pale, jutting chin. His hands were long and soft and white, like a woman's, and they dealt the cards with a deft, whispering expertise.

Watching the game with a sweaty, lusty intensity, Rose was standing behind one of the two men flanking Cheyenne, her mouth open slightly. He guessed this was the Tex she had mentioned earlier. His arm was no longer resting in a sling, which meant he was a healthy man again. He had wide shoulders, a high, narrow forehead, and blue eyes so light they were like holes in his face.

"Why all the commotion?" Longarm asked the sheriff.

"It's showdown time."

"What's the house gambler's name?"

"Ace Heller. It's just between him and Cheyenne now."

"You tell Cheyenne I'm in town?"

"He knows. Said he was glad you made it."

Longarm nodded.

Miles Pike, the one Rose accused of manhandling her, was sitting across from Tex. He hadn't shrunk any since leaving the pass. His sweaty face had a pair of chins and his tiny eyes looked like raisins sitting in bread dough. Longarm wondered how the man had been able to find a gunbelt long enough to encompass his massive belly. Len Turco was nowhere in sight.

Small leather sacks of gold dust, their strings drawn tight, were piled high in front of Cheyenne. The pot looked enormous. Apparently, Cheyenne was doing his best to break the Drovers Hall bank. A man with a black string tie appeared behind Ace, a frown on his face.

"That the owner?" Longarm asked the sheriff.

"Ben Haldeman, yeah. Right now he's a very worried man."

But Ace Heller did not seem in the least troubled. He surveyed his hand and cocked an inquiring eyebrow at the Kid. "You stayin' in?"

Cheyenne pushed forward two sacks of gold dust. "Match that."

They were playing draw poker and had finished building their hands. Cheyenne had drawn two cards, Ace three. Without batting an eye, Ace pushed out enough chips to match Cheyenne's bet, then placed an additional two hundred dollars worth of chips in alongside it.

"I'm raisin' you," he said.

Cheyenne matched the raise and raised Ace another hundred.

"We still playing table stakes?" Ace asked the saloon owner.

"Sure, Ace," the man said. "Table stakes it is."

With coldly appraising eyes Ace studied his winnings, then looked across at Cheyenne's pile of chips and gold dust.

"How much you got there, Cheyenne?" Ace asked.

"Ain't had time to count it. Say three thousand."

"That's close enough to what I got on the table," Ace said calmly, his face impassive. "If it ain't, Ben'll cover me. Ain't that right, Ben?"

"Sure, Ace. You oughta know what you're holding."

The crowded saloon became as hushed as a church as the two men pushed all they had in front of them into the enormous pot.

"All right," said Ace. "I'm callin' you, Cheyenne. What've you got?"

Cheyenne slapped his hand down, faceup. The crowd around the table surged forward, then pulled back, gasping. Cheyenne had four aces. He had won, broken the bank, closed down Drovers Hall! In the back a few men cheered cautiously as an excited buzz filled the place. Longarm heard the news being relayed to those outside in the street.

But Ace seemed not in the least perturbed. A thin, condescending smile on his face, he coolly laid down a straight flush, king high, spreading the hand neatly across the table in front of him so that all could see.

Ace Heller had Cheyenne beat!

Gasping, Rose stepped back. A startled murmur swept the saloon. That two such powerful poker hands could have been drawn in one game—with so much at stake—astounded the onlookers. It surprised Longarm as well.

In the shocked silence that fell over the poker table, Cheyenne gazed down at Ace's winning hand, his face dark with outrage. Then he looked up at Ace.

"I don't know how you did it, but that sure was neat. Straight flush, king high. Where in blazes did you get them cards?"

"You callin' me a cheat?"

"You denying it?"

As Cheyenne spoke, he drew his Colt. Ace scraped his chair back and jumped to his feet. His hand dropped to his belt and he yanked out his belly gun. Before he could fire, Cheyenne blasted him in the chest, twice. Mouth open, Ace walked stiffly backward like a wooden soldier, then toppled to the floor. Men shouted. A bar girl screamed. There was a stampede to get out of the place to avoid getting caught in the cross fire. But there were no more shots. It was over as soon as it had begun. Cheyenne's two bullets had ended the quarrel with a neat and final dispatch.

The sheriff joined Longarm beside the dead gambler.

"What's that?" Rose cried.

She was pointing to a queer contraption sticking out of Ace's sleeve. It was a metal collapsible device holding cards in a metal clip at one end. Longarm knew immediately what it was—a sleeve holdout. Strapped to Ace's arm, it had enabled Ace to extend a playing card into his waiting palm whenever he needed one. To activate it, all he had to do was bend his elbow. When the arm was straightened, a rubber band retracted the metal clip.

As the dead gambler was carried from the saloon, Cheyenne walked over to the table to gather up his loot. When Ben Haldeman started to protest, Cheyenne asked him loudly—making sure that everyone in the place heard him—how in the hell Ace Heller could have been using a sleeve holdout all this time without him knowing it. Ben Haldeman promptly shut up. Tex and Miles Pike cleaned off the table for Cheyenne, then went over to the window to cash up.

As they did so, Longarm and the sheriff approached Cheyenne.

"Howdy, Longarm," Cheyenne said. "Ham told me you got away from them two assholes."

"It wasn't easy."

"I didn't think it would be."

"How'd you do it, Cheyenne?" the sheriff asked. "How'd you know Ace was cheating."

"His cuffs."

"His cuffs? What do you mean?"

"They were too wide."

"I got to run you out now, Cheyenne. Sorry. But you just killed a man."

"Ace went for his belly gun. You saw it. Everyone in town saw it."

"You drew first."

Tex and Miles Pike pulled up beside Cheyenne. "We got it all, Kid," Tex said.

"All right," Cheyenne said. Then he looked at the

65

sheriff. "Have it your way, Ham. Looks like I wore this town out anyway."

With a curt nod to Longarm, Cheyenne left them and escorted his two heavily-laden gang members from the place.

Back in his hotel room after a few more beers, Longarm didn't bother to light the lamp on his dresser. He jammed his chair up against the door knob, tucked his Colt under the pillow, then quickly undressed and dropped heavily onto the bed, his right hand closed over the Colt's grips. He was almost asleep when he heard a soft footfall approaching the bed.

He was awake instantly, his Colt swinging out from under the pillow.

"Don't shoot!" Rose cried.

"What the hell!"

"I had to see you!"

"How'd you get in here?"

"You left the door open. I was waiting in here for you, but I fell asleep in the corner."

Longarm shoved his .44 back under the pillow, then lit the lamp on his dresser to get a better look at Rose. She slumped into an upholstered rocker beside Longarm's bed, her hands clasped in her lap. She looked very dejected.

"What do you want, Rose?"

"Comfort," she pouted. "If you think you can manage it."

"For what?"

"The gang's leaving—and Cheyenne says I can't go with them."

"What does Tex say?"

"He says anything Cheyenne wants is okay with him."

"So you stay here."

"I don't want to."

"Then go back to your husband."

"Jack?"

"Unless you have others you haven't told me about."

"I'll never go back to him."

"He loves you."

"Is that what you call it? Love from a man like that makes me feel like a maggot."

Longarm sighed wearily. "What do you want me to do?"

"I already told you. I want you . . . comfort me. You treat me nice. You aren't like them other animals."

"When is Cheyenne pulling out?"

"Tomorrow."

"Then I'll have to go after them. Best thing for you is to stay here and keep out of the way. You might get caught in the cross fire."

"You mean you're goin' against all four?"

"I'll be very careful."

"You are either a fool or a very brave man."

"Maybe I'm both."

She got up from the rocker. "I said I like you. Let me prove it."

She pushed him gently back down onto the bed and kissed him on the lips, hard. He found it impossible not to respond. She stepped out of her dress. He had been right. There was nothing much under it. In a moment, her pale, naked body glowing in the lamp's soft light, she joined him on the bed. With practiced ease, her hot fingers found his growing erection and with an eager sigh, she swung aboard him.

"Yes," she purred. "Me on top, you on the bottom. I am no missionary and you are no priest. Did you know this is how the Romans did it? I will ride you like I ride a horse."

"Take it easy. Don't bend that. It's the only one I got."

"I will not break him, I promise. I will go slow at first. Then you must hang on."

"I done this sort of thing before, Rose. Just shut up and get on with it."

She sat back down on him recklessly, impaling herself with a hearty disregard for his vulnerability. Then she wriggled her behind a little more to settle him still deeper into her until he was enveloped clear to the base of his shaft by her moist, enclosing warmth. She began to rock then, slowly.

Laboring happily, she looked down at him as if from a great height, smiling, beads of perspiration standing out on her cheeks and forehead, the tip of her tongue running back and forth along her parted lips. Pleasuring him was pleasing her as well, it appeared. He leaned back and let nature take its course, thrusting eagerly up to meet her downward thrusts until he found himself roaring into the homestretch. He saw her face harden into a grimace of pleasure. By now they were melded into one single passionate entity. He crossed the finish line, exploding under her, feeling himself gushing deep into her. Eyes squeezed tightly shut, she flung her head back and climaxed with a violence that surprised him. He heard her gasping shriek, and then she was leaning forward onto him, her breasts slamming into his face, her fists beating wildly on his chest . . .

The tumult subsided. She rolled off him, panting slightly.

"Mmmm," she said. "That was nice."

"I got no complaints."

"You want seconds?"

"Hold off a minute, will you? I'm bushed. You can really hang a man out to dry."

"You mean I can stay in here with you?"

"Sure. But I'll be gettin' up at sunup."

"I'll wake you."

He chuckled. "I'll bet you will."

She giggled, pulled the sheet over her shoulder, and snuggled closer to him. He did not blow out the lamp, but reached up to make sure his .44 was still where he'd left it under the pillow, then closed his hand around the walnut grips and shut his eyes.

And waited.

At last he heard the pause in Rose's steady breathing. After a moment she slipped with infinite care out from under the sheets and dressed. Her shoes in her hand, she padded silently to the door. She was so careful and patient as she removed the back of the chair from under the doorknob, he didn't hear a thing. Soft footsteps sounded in the hallway, pausing just outside the door. Rose turned the knob. That he could hear. As she pulled the door open, he rolled off the bed.

Rose saw him.

"Watch out!" she cried as the four men rushed past her into the room. "He's awake!"

From under the bed he saw the legs of the four outlaws

as they pulled up in front of the bed and poured lead into it. Longarm cut loose himself, and saw one man stagger and go down. As the other three turned and bolted from the room, a stick of dynamite struck the floor and rolled toward him, its fuse sparkling like a Chinese firecracker. As Rose and Cheyenne vanished out the door, Longarm scrambled from under the bed, picked up the stick, and flung it through the doorway as Rose and the outlaws plunged down the stairs. The sputtering dynamite struck the wall above the stairs, then dropped out of sight.

A second later a titanic explosion reverberated in the stairwell. Longarm heard the ring of balustrades breaking loose, and almost lost his balance as the floor under him shook violently. The lamp skittered off the dresser and crashed onto the rug. He put out the flames with the blanket and ran out of the room. Peering over the railing, he saw one of the outlaws sprawled facedown at the bottom. He hurried back into his room to get dressed, ignoring the outlaw he had shot who was crumpled beside the door, then ran down the stairs to see who'd been caught by the blast. When he got to the man's side, the sheriff was bending over the sprawled figure, while on the landing below the shocked owner of the hotel, dressed in a long white nightshirt, looked up at them, his face as white as the nightshirt he was wearing.

The sheriff turned the outlaw over. There was a gasp from those above looking over the railing. The dead man's head was attached to his shoulder by a single bloody strip of flesh and his face looked as if it had been through a meat-grinder. Despite the mutilation, however, there was no doubt which one this was.

Len Turco, the mad dynamiter.

"What the hell's going on here?" the sheriff asked Longarm.

"This here's the one I got the warrant for, the one I told you about. Len Turco. The poor son of a bitch tried to blow me up. Looks like he was hoist by his own petard."

The sheriff frowned. "Petard, you say?"

"It's an expression."

"Well, I can verify what you say, I guess. I been hearing talk this one carried dynamite in his saddlebags."

"There's another one upstairs in my bedroom."

"One of Cheyenne's men?"

Longarm nodded.

"Jesus. Let's take a look."

The sheriff preceded Longarm up the stairs. Night-shirted guests were crowding around his room's open doorway. Farnum brushed past them, then pulled up to gaze down at the unconscious outlaw. One look at the downed man's bulk and Longarm knew it had to be Miles Pike. Farnum nudged the big body over onto its back.

"Goddamn," the sheriff muttered. "Look at that dirty hole in his gut. Pike's going to be real unhappy when he wakes up."

"Better get the doctor."

"Yeah."

As the sheriff left the room, Longarm finished dressing and lugged his gear downstairs and across the street to the livery stable. The stench of Pike's wound hung over his room like a curse. Besides, this way he could get an early start in the morning.

Chapter 6

At sunup Longarm knocked on the back door to Mr. Wong's tailor shop. The little man pulled the door open almost immediately, and looking past him at the undisturbed cot, Longarm realized that the tailor had been working through the night.

"Ah, yes," Mr. Wong said, bowing his head quickly. "All finish. Much work. Next time, you take better care."

Longarm stepped into the shop, took off what he was wearing, and climbed into his brown tweed trousers. The shirt had been mended neatly, washed, and then pressed dry. He slipped on the vest, and when he fastened the derringer to the watch chain and dropped it into the fob pocket, it fit perfectly. He shrugged into the brown tweed frock coat and judged it to be almost as good as new.

He paid the tailor what he asked, then doubled the amount, in grateful appreciation of his extra effort.

Longarm returned to the livery stable, packed the old clothes he had been wearing in his saddle roll, then went back to the hotel and asked the desk clerk for Rose's room number.

She answered his first knock.

"Who's there!" she cried, her voice close to panic.

"Longarm."

"Don't you dare come in here! I have a gun!"

He placed his left foot against the door alongside the knob, then pushed. With a crunch of splitting wood, the door swung open. He strode in. Rose was on the bed, a gun in her hand.

"I'll shoot!"

He kept on, and when he got close enough he reached out and twisted the gun out of her hand. She scrunched up against the headboard and flung up her arms to protect herself from the blows she expected.

Longarm emptied the Colt's load onto the bedspread, then flung the empty gun across the room onto a soft chair. He sat down on the edge of the bed and waited for Rose to lower her arms. When she did, what he saw this close shocked him. She had been beaten ruthlessly about the face and neck. Her lips were split and swollen, one eye was nearly closed, and he saw a raw, painful-looking bruise on her shoulder.

"Go ahead," she said. "Why don't you start on me too."

"Looks like I don't have to. Someone's already taken care of that chore for me. Rose, you set me up."

"It was Tex. He made me."

"Oh?"

74

"He said if I did it, he'd talk the Kid into taking me with them."

"You must want to go with them real bad."

She shuddered and hugged her shoulders. "Anything is better than staying here and working in that dive across the street." She peered at him closely. "You don't look so mad at me. Ain't you?"

"I am, don't worry. But then I have to confess, I wasn't entirely surprised when you opened that door."

"You mean you knew all along?"

"Let's say I was pretty sure of what you were up to— you and Cheyenne."

"Then why did you let me do it?"

"I figured if I acted fast enough, I might be able to whittle the Kid's gang down some."

"Well, you sure did that, all right."

"The stable boy said he heard Cheyenne and Tex ride out last night."

"Yes. Right after the explosion."

"Which way are they going, Rose?"

"How would I know that?"

"Don't go dumb on me."

"I don't know what you're talking about. They never let me in on their secrets. They tell me as little as they can."

"I don't believe that."

"Believe what you like."

"Look, Rose. You're at a dead end here. You know that. I can help you."

"Help me? How?"

"On my way back, I'll stop here and take you with me, drop you off at the ranch."

"You mean take me back to Jack?"

"Think about it. Could it be any worse than this?"

"You're crazy if you think I'd go back with him."

Longarm shrugged and got up off the bed and started for the door. Before he reached it, she asked him to hold up. He turned to face her. She had a frown on her face, and it was clear she was considering his words—and her alternatives. She didn't really have all that many, and it was clear she was beginning to realize this.

"Well?" he prodded.

"I'm thinkin'," she snapped. "I'm thinkin'."

"That's a good sign," he said, returning to the bed.

"All I can tell you is what I overheard."

"What did you overhear?"

"On the way, they'll maybe visit a ranch north of here in the mountains."

"Who runs it?"

"A man called Clampett."

"He's a cattleman?"

"He makes moonshine, I heard."

"I see. A rural businessman."

"I guess so."

"How far is this place?"

"Tex said four to five days ride, but it could be longer. I'm not sure."

"You said, 'On the way.' Where they heading after Clampett's?"

"I don't know."

Longarm started for the door again.

"You goin' after them now?"

Longarm halted and turned to face her. "That's right."

"Well . . . don't forget what you promised."

76

"You mean you'll go back with me—willingly—to Jack Collins and his ranch?"

Tears streaming down her cheeks, she nodded, doing her best to keep herself from breaking into sobs.

He left her room, and ten minutes later rode out.

Four days later, deep in the mountains, Longarm selected a campsite by a stream and dismounted. It was only noon, but already he was saddle-weary. He watered the black, filled his canteen, and was sitting with his back to a pine, trying to get himself comfortable, when he thought he heard someone pulling himself across pine needles toward him.

Slowly, carefully, he drew his .44. Pretending to be asleep, he rested his head back against the tree, cradling the Colt out of sight in his lap. The sound grew louder. It was unmistakably that of someone slipping over pine needles and brush, heading straight for him. He waited until the last possible moment, then rolled away from the tree and jumped up. A man he had never seen before— dressed in torn buckskins and a ragged cotton shirt—left the ground in a leap at him, a huge bowie knife flashing in his right hand.

Longarm parried the knife thrust with his Colt but was unable to prevent his attacker from driving him backward down a small slope. His heel caught an exposed root and he went down heavily, his attacker atop him. The man's knife flashed down, but Longarm was able to parry the blow and roll out of his grasp. Before his attacker could lunge at him again, Longarm clipped the man on the side of his head with the barrel of his Colt. It was a desperate but well-timed blow. With a grunt, Longarm's attacker sagged to his knees, the knife dropping from his fingers.

Longarm clubbed the man again. The fellow collapsed facedown onto the ground. Longarm rolled him over and straddled him, his knees pinning the man's arms. Then he grabbed the man's thick shock of hair, pulled his head off the ground, and slammed it back down. He did this twice before he got his attacker's complete attention. As the man's eyes flew open, Longarm smiled down at him and pressed the muzzle of his Colt against his Adam's apple. The fellow said nothing, closed his eyes, and waited stoically for Longarm's bullet to crash through his windpipe.

"You son of a bitch," Longarm said to him. "Give me one good reason why I shouldn't pull this trigger."

"I can't," the fellow managed. "I can't think of a single one."

"Who the hell are you anyway?"

"Jed Tumbrill."

"What's the matter with you, Jed? How come you attacked me like that?"

"I figured you had a horse and a gun. And I need both."

"Why?"

"It's a long story. You mind lifting that gun barrel a mite? It's tickling my Adam's apple every time I speak."

Longarm pulled the gun back a few inches. He was pissed. This son of a bitch had probably put his trousers and frock coat right back to where they had been when he rode into Gallstone.

"Well?"

"The Clampetts are after me."

"The Clampetts, you say?"

"I went there with my woman to get married. Old Man Clampett's the only preacher hereabouts. But while we were there, two riders rode in and one of them took a shine to my woman."

"So you protested."

"And so did she."

"What'd you do?"

"I tried to take my woman away. But they got her back and went after me."

"What were going to do when you got my horse and weapon?"

"Go back after the bastards. What do you think?"

"Alone?"

"That don't matter. I got to free my woman."

Longarm smiled, holstered his .44, then pulled Jed Tumbrill to his feet.

"You won't need to go back after the Clampetts alone. I'll go with you."

"What are you up to, mister? You in league with the Clampetts?"

"Not on your life. I'm interested in them two you said rode into their place. One of them was called Tex and the other the Kid. Right?"

"Yeah. The Cheyenne Kid. But it wasn't him caused the trouble. It was the feller with him. Tex."

"Cheyenne and Tex still there?"

"They was last I knew."

"What's your woman's name?"

"Black Dove. She's a Flathead. But that don't mean her head's flat. Fact is, she's the prettiest thing I ever saw. So, who're you anyway?"

Longarm took out his wallet and flashed his badge. "My friends call me Longarm."

"My God, a U. S. federal marshal. I sure as hell know how to pick 'em, don't I? I'm tellin' you, Longarm, this here bein' a mountain man ain't all it's cracked up to be."

"Not like in them dime novels, eh?"

Jed nodded somberly. "It don't say nothing in them books about the beaver all bein' trapped out, or how long the winters are, or how lonely it can get without a woman."

"Where you from, Jed?"

"St. Louis. I come here three years ago."

"Okay. That's it then. Show me the way to the Clampetts' place. But we'll have to ride double."

"I don't mind."

"How far is it?"

"Ten miles."

"Let's go," Longarm told him. "It'll be close to dark when we get there and that might be a help."

Before he started for his black, Longarm noted that this time—despite his brawl with the young mountain man—his trousers and frock coat were still in reasonable condition. The pine needles had been slick enough to prevent them from catching onto anything sharp or jagged.

He was thankful for small blessings.

As Longarm had figured, it was close to dusk when they came on the Clampett ranch. Leaving the black tethered to a sapling in the timber behind them, Longarm and Jed stole to the edge of the flat fronting the ranch compound, and ducked into some brush. They decided to wait for nightfall before moving in any closer.

The ranch buildings were planted in among cotton-wood and pine. Even from this distance the smell of mash hung in the air. The main building was a log affair, and behind it was another shedlike building, where Clampett probably kept his still. Beyond the horse barn were corrals leading into a lush, spring-fed meadow. Longarm glimpsed sleek, well-conditioned saddle horses high-stepping in the distance. Evidently Clampett's moonshining enterprise was doing well.

Abruptly, the ground behind them reverberated with the pound of hooves. They glanced back to see two riders emerge from the trees behind them. Dismounting on the run, the riders ducked low and began to run through the tall grass toward them. One of them was taller and heftier than the other.

"Will and Benjy Clampett," whispered Jed. "They seen us."

"And now we've seen them."

"Yeah," Jed said, taking out his knife. "Will's that little one, a real mean bastard. His brother Benjy's not as mean, but he's trouble all the same."

"Keep low. Maybe we can take them without firing a shot."

The two brothers had evidently been in the woodland when Longarm and Jed rode up, and were now hoping to spring on them unawares; the only thing was they had been as stealthy as a herd of stampeding buffalo. Longarm could hear them flattening vines and snapping dried twigs as they crept closer.

"All right, you two," Will cried, bursting on them. "We got you covered."

Jed leaped to his feet and charged Will, his knife slashing wildly. Falling back in terror, Will fired wildly at Jed, then went down. Jed kicked the gun out of his hands just as Longarm spun over and fired up at Will's big brother, catching him in the forearm. Benjy dropped his gun and sank to one knee, holding onto his arm. Tears exploded from his eyes and coursed down his oxlike face, an almost comical sight in a man so big. Meanwhile Jed had hauled Will back onto his feet. Longarm snatched up Benjy's gun and tossed it aside as Jed snatched up Will's gun and stuck it in his belt.

"What do we do now?" Jed asked warily, glancing at the ranch buildings across the flat. "Someone over there must've heard them shots."

"You want your Indian woman back. I want Cheyenne. Now we got two hostages to make the head of this clan turn them in to us."

"I don't know," said Jed, shaking his head doubtfully. "You don't know John Clampett like I do."

"These *are* his sons?"

"Yep."

"Well, then."

"It ain't as simple as that, Longarm. He's a wild man. He lives on the moonshine he makes, but he ain't just a moonshiner. When he mood hits him, he calls himself a preacher of God's Word."

"Oh, shit. One of those."

At that moment, Longarm saw someone emerge from the ranch house, a rifle in his hand. Even from this distance Longarm could see how tall and rangy the fellow was, his face covered with a dark thatch of a beard. He paused on the low porch, shading his eyes as he peered across the flat. Then he stepped off the porch and started toward them. Three ranch hands, also lugging rifles, boiled out of the bunkhouse to back Clampett. Longarm saw no sign of Cheyenne or Tex, and figured they were holed up in the cabin, covering Clampett.

"Here comes Clampett," Jed said nervously.

"We're ready for them," said Longarm.

He hauled the wounded Benjy to his feet and planted him in front of him. Beside him, a very nervous Jed pushed Will in front of him as well.

"Ready?" Longarm asked Jed.

"Not really."

The two, pushing their hostages in front of them, advanced to meet Clampett and his three ranch hands. As he neared Clampett, Longarm saw he was lean enough to dance in a rifle barrel. His wrists were long and slender, as were his fingers. His cheekbones and forehead had been turned almost black by the sun, and his eyes, peering out of deep hollows, were dark blue and had an almost hypnotic intensity.

"Hold it right there, Clampett," Longarm said, when he judged Clampett was close enough. "You and your men come any closer and we'll blast your boys. Our gun barrels are resting on their spines right now."

Clampett halted, his eyes flashing contemptuously at his two sons. The three ranch hands halted a few feet behind him.

"Lower them guns," Longarm said. "All of you."

Grudgingly they lowered their rifles.

Ignoring Longarm and Jed, Clampett fastened his dark

eyes on his two sons. They were filled not only with contempt—but loathing.

"You two done me agin," he seethed. "Not a one of you is worth a pinch of coon shit! How come you let these two take you!"

"It weren't our fault, Pa," pleaded Will. "They tricked us."

"You mean they fought back—that it?"

"Pa," cried Benjy. "Lookit me. I'm wounded! This one put a slug in my arm."

"Serves you right for lettin' him get the drop on you!"

"Pa! It hurts."

"That's it, you whipped curl. Snivel! That's all you're good for."

"Leave him be, Pa," said Will. "He's hurt bad."

"That's right, Pa!" cried Benjy. "I'm hurt bad!"

"If you can stand, you ain't hurt. Stop that snivelin'."

Clampett turned his full attention on Longarm. "Who the hell're you, mister?"

"I'm a deputy U. S. marshal. I'm after the Cheyenne Kid. I heard he's at your ranch. Send him and his sidekick out now. And Jed's woman too."

"Can't do that. Cheyenne and Tex rode out this noon with Black Dove."

"I don't believe you."

"I don't much care if you do." He grinned at Longarm. "Cheyenne told me you might show up." He sent a long arrow of tobacco juice into the ground, then wiped his beard off with the back of his hand. "He gave me a retainer, you might say, to keep you here. Permanent."

The three ranch hands standing behind Clampett

snickered, their yellow teeth gleaming like fangs.

Longarm said, "All right, drop your weapons and move back across the flat."

"And if we don't?"

"We'll gun both your boys down right in front of you."

Clampett laughed. "You wouldn't do that. You're a U.S. marshal. Lawmen don't gun down fools like my two boys here. It ain't in their nature. And if you do, we'll just cut you down. And you know I mean it." He looked coldly at Jed. "Ain't that right, Jed?"

Jed glanced at Longarm, then back at Clampett. He nodded unhappily. "I guess so."

"Besides," Clampett said, "what makes you think I give a damn if you kill these two whelps? I might even be grateful. It'd mean I got two less mouths to feed."

"Pa!" cried Benjy. "Don't talk like that!"

Clampett strode angrily up to his son and slapped him so hard the young man spun halfway around, then sank to the ground. Before Longarm and Jed could react, Clampett whirled on them, his rifle trained on them both. At the same time, the three ranch hands surrounded them, rifles cocked and ready.

"I'll take that Colt," Clampett said to Longarm.

Longarm handed it to him. Jed handed Will's gun back to him. At once Will turned on Jed and punched him in the gut. As Jed knifed over, Will brought the gun barrel down, catching Jed on the top of his head. Jed staggered, but managed somehow to stay upright. Benjy, hugging his wounded arm, got slowly to his feet.

"Let's go," said Clampett, waggling his rifle barrel at Longarm and Jed.

When they reached the compound, two women burst from the cabin. One of them, having seen that Benjy had been wounded, began winding a bandage around his wound even before he reached the cabin. Will followed his brother and the two women into the cabin.

"Clampett," Jed said bitterly, "I want that money back I gave you!"

"I ain't refunding you no money. I kept my part of the deal. I married you two, all legal and proper. It ain't my fault your woman took a shine to Tex."

"She didn't take no shine to Tex. He forced himself on her."

Clampett smiled. "You can believe that if you want to."

Clampett turned to the three hands. "Show these two to that feed room in the horse barn. That should hold them. And they can have all they feed they can eat."

The three men grinned.

As they started off with Longarm and Jed, Clampett told one of them to get a chair and keep on guard outside the door after they trussed them up. "I don't want these two gettin' loose." He glanced up at the sky. "There's goin' to be a full moon tonight—a good night for coon hunting."

The one he addressed broke into a grin. "Come on, you big coon," he told Longarm, rapping him smartly on the side of his head with his rifle stock. "Head for the barn."

As Longarm started up, the other two booted Jed

86

unceremoniously after him. Since Clampett had not taken Longarm's derringer, he appreciated the wisdom of protesting no further and allowed himself to be bullied across the compound toward the horse barn.

Chapter 7

The ranch hand did not do a very good job of tying them up. As soon as he locked them in the grain room and took his post outside the door, Longarm and Jed promptly maneuvered around so that each could untie the other's wrists, after which they approached the flimsy door and took turns trying to peer out through the single crack that ran down its middle. The guard had lit a lantern and hung it on a nail alongside the door.

The back of the guard's head was clearly visible as he sat in front of the door, his Winchester leaning stock down against the wall beside him. Longarm and Jed conferred softly. They would break through the door and disarm the guard. The door was so flimsy, this should not be too difficult, both agreed.

They moved back from the door. Longarm was the bigger, so he was the one assigned the task of bursting through first. Jed would follow and help him overpower the guard. The thing was they had to do all this in a big hurry, without letting the guard get off a shot—or they'd alert the house.

"Ready?" Longarm asked Jed.

Jed nodded.

Longarm stood up and took a few steps back to get himself a good start. Jed crouched beside him. But before Longarm could move, the front legs of the guard's chair came down hard, his boots striking the floor loudly. Two quick shots from his rifle sent slugs through the door. It was a miracle neither Longarm or Jed was hit as both flung themselves to the floor.

"Hey, you two in there," the guard said, chuckling. "Keep still. Next time I hear you moving around, I'll turn this door into a sieve."

Flat on the floor, Longarm turned his head and looked at Jed. "I think he means it."

Jed nodded.

Slowly, carefully, the two men scrunched up to the wall on either side of the door. Longarm realized they would have to devise a different scheme, and the hardcase outside the door had already provided it. Reaching up, Longarm tapped the door, then shook it slightly. At once the fellow blasted two more holes in the door.

"Jesus," said Jed. "You're gonna get us killed."

Ignoring him, Longarm tapped the door again, initiating a third fusillade. This time there were dim shouts from the ranch house, and a moment later someone tramped into the barn.

"What the hell's goin' on?" the newcomer demanded.

"That's Ned, another son," Jed whispered.

Their guard explained that he was keeping his captives

down so they wouldn't try to break out.

"Well, shit," Ned told him. "You kill them two, we ain't goin to have no fun tonight."

"Don't worry, Ned. They'll be ready."

Ned tramped out of the barn.

"That Ned's the favorite," Jed told Longarm softly.

"What's so special about him?"

"He's the youngest and the apple of the old bastard's eye. Blond, blue-eyed, and knows how to suck ass. It's sickening to watch him play up to the old pirate."

"What's all this about coon hunting tonight."

"You ain't goin' to like this."

"Try me."

"There's been some talk. Clampett and his boys like to hunt."

"Nothing unusual about that."

"It's *what* they like to hunt."

"It ain't coons then."

"It's people. Humans. Most of the time anyone they catch trying to steal their moonshine."

"And we're it this time."

"No question."

"He has dogs?"

"Three hounds. They're good trackers."

"I think we'd better get the hell out of here."

"Sure. But how—with that madman outside the door?"

Longarm smiled. "I think I've already taken care of that."

"What're you talkin' about?"

"Shhh . . ."

Their guard got up from his seat and they could see

his shadow moving in front of the crack in the door, then blocking it out entirely as he pressed his ear against the door. He was suspicious at their whispering and was listening closely, trying to figure what they were up to. Longarm waited until the guard returned to his chair. When he tipped it back against the door, Longarm withdrew the derringer from his vest pocket.

He smiled at the astonishment on Jed's face.

"You see?" he whispered. "With all that gunfire I provoked, one more gunshot won't even raise an eyebrow."

Reaching up, Longarm pressed the upper barrel of the derringer into the crack just behind the guard's head—and pulled the trigger, the detonation deafening in the tiny grain room. The guard crashed forward to the floor.

"Put your shoulder down," Longarm told Jed. "We still got to break out of here."

At the count of three, both men hurled themselves at the door. They broke through it so easily, Jed went flying over the chair. Longarm snatched up the guard's Winchester and searched through his pockets for extra shells as Jed strapped the guard's gunbelt about his waist. Longarm went to the open barn door and peered out.

The full moon was riding high in the night sky, imparting to the pine-clad mountains a luminous blue clarity. Abruptly, the silence of the night was broken by the eager baying of hounds and the cries of men urging them on. The sound came rapidly closer.

"Here they come," Jed said.

"Let's get the hell out of here," Longarm said, breaking out of the barn and heading for the timber.

• • •

Once in the timber, they split.

Jed headed north while Longarm kept on straight, intending to circle around to pick up his black, assuming it had remained where he had tethered it. He had not gone far before he heard the hounds break into two packs. Two dogs seemed to be moving after Jed, while only one was attempting to overtake him. Longarm increased his pace. Ahead of him he glimpsed a ridge on the far side of a moonlit flat. He cut across it and clambered up into the rocks fronting the ridge. He rested the rifle on a flat rock in front of him and peered into the timber he had just left, waiting for the hound to break into the clear.

He didn't have long to wait.

Still leashed to its handler, the hound plunged out of the timber, its tail wagging excitedly, its muzzle to the ground when it was not baying. There were two men plunging after the handler. One of them, the tallest, was John Clampett, his companion a slight towhead who was sticking close beside him. This would be Ned.

Clampett pulled up and Longarm heard him shout at the handler to pull in the hound. But the animal was almost beside himself by this time and could not be restrained. With a ferocious lunge, it stripped the leash out of its handler's grasp and baying joyously, raced across the flat, heading straight for Longarm's position in the rocks. The three men raced out onto the flat in a futile attempt to overtake the hound. Longarm tucked the stock into his shoulder and tracked the hound, his sights on the dog's head. When it got to within twenty yards of the rocks—despite a deep reluctance—he squeezed the trigger. The dog yelped and rolled over, dead on the instant.

Longarm stood up then and took aim at Clampett, who—along with his son and the handler—was caught flat-footed in the middle of the moonlit flat. Clampett turned about and ran toward the timber, dragging his son after him, the handler pulling up the rear. As Clampett ran he sent wild, rapid fire back at Longarm. Longarm paid the futile barrage no mind as he tracked the dog's handler and squeezed off a shot. The man took a few stumbling strides forward, then buckled and went down. Longarm sent his next round after Clampett. He thought he saw the man stagger a moment before he disappeared with Ned into the timber.

Longarm waited a moment longer, then clambered down out of the rocks and trotted into the timber bordering the flat. Without their hound, Clampett's coon hunt was over for now. But only for now. Longarm reached the timber and kept on into it, grateful for the brilliant moon hanging above, and was well pleased to find his black where he had tethered it. There were signs aplenty of the horse's unhappiness at such a long wait without water, and a pile of horse manure to emphasize the point. Longarm did not mount him; instead he led him back through the timber to a stream he remembered crossing earlier that afternoon. When he reached it, both he and the horse drank their fill.

Then Longarm mounted up and spurred after the faint cry of baying hounds. From the sound of it, Jed was still on the move, still ahead of his hunters. But that would not be for long.

By closing in relentlessly on the sound, Longarm

emerged onto a ridge not long after and saw below him Jed plunging across a shallow stream. At the same time, from a line of timber a few hundred feet further down the ravine, bolted Benjy, Will, and one of the ranch hands. Because of his wound, Benjy was letting the ranch hand and Will handle the two hounds.

As Jed clambered up onto the stream's opposite bank, Will got off a quick, desperate shot. A portion of the embankment close beside Jed erupted. Jed kept going and dove into a pile of rocks above the stream, and almost immediately returned fire with his Colt. At that distance his Colt was not very deadly, but it was enough to give his pursuers pause. They had not figured on their coons firing back at them.

Stupidly, Will and the ranch hand released the dogs and sent them after Jed. Jed held his fire until the dogs splashed into the stream. Then he fired. One dog spun, yelping, as the bullet plowed into his flank. Undaunted, the other one piled up onto the farthest bank and started for the rocks. Jed fired again. The hound was caught in the chest. It flopped over and then, whining piteously, began to drag itself still further toward the rocks.

Longarm clapped his heels to the black and slanted swiftly down off the ridge, opening up on Will and the others with his rifle, levering rapidly. Already disheartened by the loss of their hounds, the three men did not return Longarm's fire with any consistency, and as Longarm rode into their midst, still firing, they scattered. Benjy stopped and hauled up a shotgun. Longarm sent a round at him quickly. Benjy spun to the ground. Spurring past him, Longarm tried to overtake Will and the ranch hand. But once they plunged into the timber, he reined up. No chance of catching them in that tangle of brush and woodland aboard a horse.

He rode back to Benjy to see what he could do to help him. He had a feeling it was more than a flesh wound the big fellow had suffered this time. But as he approached the downed man, Benjy flung up a six-gun and got off two quick shots. Both rounds missed Longarm, but came so close he thought he could hear their swift, hot passage. He flung himself off his horse, landed on his feet, and pumped four rounds into the young Clampett.

He moved closer to the bleeding piece of earth. One look told him how completely the young man had been killed. His desperate, foolhardy attempt to blow a hole in Longarm even though he'd been cut down was no doubt his way of proving to himself—and to his pa—that he wasn't just a sniveler.

Longarm looked up and saw Jed hopping down from the rocks. He mounted up and rode across the stream to meet him. Jed was looking down at the dead hounds.

"I hated to do that," Jed said.

"From the look of them, they were damned good trackers," Longarm commented. "I don't see you had much choice."

"What do we do now?"

"I don't know about you, Jed. I'm going back to the Clampett place."

"My God, man, why?"

"I got to deliver a corpse."

"You're taking Benjy back? Why?"

"I want Old Man Clampett to know what can happen when he plays these kinds of games. Besides, he's taken my double-action Colt .44-40. What are your plans?"

"See that peak over there?"

Longarm nodded.

"Just beyond is a cabin belongs to a mountain man friend of mine. Ike Callahan. He's got a cabin sets on a ridge overlooking the valley. I'll rest there awhile and then go after Black Dove. No one's goin' to tell me she went with Tex willingly."

"Don't be in too much of a hurry. Wait there for me."

"Sure. I'll wait. But not forever."

"I won't take long. Now give me a hand with Benjy."

Jed swung up behind Longarm and they rode back across the stream. It was a grisly task, but Jed did not shrink as he helped fling the dead Clampett over the horse's back and tie him down. Longarm mounted up then, and watched Jed splash across the stream. Jed turned when he gained the far bank, waved good-bye, and disappeared beyond the rocks.

Longarm tethered the black to a corral post behind Clampett's barn, then lugged the dead Benjy in through the back door. He grabbed a pitchfork, took it outside to a spot beside the entrance, and plunged its tines deep into the ground; then he went back inside for Benjy's body and propped it up upon the pitchfork's handle. Since Clampett took pleasure in hunting his fellow humans, perhaps this grisly reminder would give him food for thought.

Longarm headed then for the ranch house. What sounded like a wail came from inside. And well it might, Longarm mused, as he reached the cabin's outside wall. He moved along it to a window. Peering into the cabin, he saw a very young woman crying with her head down on the table. Benjy's sister, he figured. Ned, two ranch hands, and Will were hovering close about the wounded Clampett, who was sitting on a chair by the sink, his left shoulder being bandaged by an older woman, maybe his wife. It must have taken some time for her to remove the bullet and staunch the bleeding, judging from the tangle of bloodstained bandages overflowing a bucket on the floor beside him.

Will's voice came clearly through the window. He was trying to convince his father to wait until daybreak before going after Benjy. But John Clampett was adamant. He was going to ride out as soon as he could mount up again.

Longarm kept on past the window, heading for the building he had earlier assumed contained Clampett's still. A large door in the rear was slightly ajar. He pulled it open all the way and stepped inside. At once he was assaulted by the pungent odor of fresh mash. Taking down a lantern hanging from a nail, he lit it, keeping the flame as low as possible. Holding it high over his head and moving it about, he took in four oversized stills huddled along the far wall. They were entangled in coils of copper tubing that seemed to have no beginning and no end. Along the wall opposite were stacked close to thirty wooden casks. Earthenware jugs were scattered everywhere. Firewood was piled in one corner.

Longarm turned the flame up as high as it would go and hurled the lamp against the wood pile. The flaming kerosene leaped over the wood, engulfing it instantly. Swiftly the flames spread across the littered floor to the casks. There was another lamp hanging from a nail close by. He plucked it down and without bothering to light it, flung it against the casks. At once great sheets of fire leapt up the casks to the beamed ceiling, then reached hungrily for the rafters.

The heat was intense. He held up his arm to protect his face and ducked out of the building, cut swiftly through the night, and found cover in some pines. He crouched down and waited. It was not long before the flames broke through the roof. As they roared higher, their garish light turned the ground around the building as bright as day.

A cry came from the cabin as the sister rushed out and pointed to the blazing roof. Will, Ned, John Clampett, and the others piled out after her. When Clampett saw the flames, the shock was so great, he grabbed hold of a porch post to steady himself. But he recovered quickly and began shouting orders. Will and the others raced back into the house for buckets, filled them at the trough pump, then raced toward the flaming building to form a pitifully short and utterly futile bucket brigade.

Longarm cut back through the pines, circled the compound, and slipped into the cabin. He found his Colt on the mantle, checked its load, then snatched up what .44-40 shells he could find and dropped them into his frock coat's side pocket. Outside the cabin, he heard footsteps pounding through the night toward him and ducked around the corner and slipped into the bunkhouse. He crouched down by a window and waited. The pounding footsteps belonged to Ned and Will. The two were running toward the barn—for more buckets, Longarm figured.

He winced when he saw the two brothers pull up in front of the barn and see what Longarm had left there.

He cursed aloud. He had wanted John Clampett to be the first to see Benjy, not these two. They turned, wailing in anger and despair, and ran back through the night to tell Clampett.

As soon as they were out of sight, Longarm left the bunkhouse, darted through the barn to his black tethered behind it, and galloped off, the night sky behind him filled with a bright, leaping glow.

Chapter 8

Longarm camped that night by a mountain stream, then kept on toward the peak Jed had pointed out to him. Late that afternoon, he glimpsed Ike's cabin perched on a ridge high above him. He cut through the timber toward it until he came upon the trail leading up to it. As he rode up the steep trail, the cabin vanished behind a great slab of rock. He kept on. After a while he heard the cool rush of a stream far below him and glimpsed its bright, mottled surface through the pines. Bird song echoed about him in the timber. Near the crest, the sod-roofed cabin broke once again into the clear, wood smoke coiling out of its chimney. When he reached the narrow clearing on which the cabin sat, a tall Rip Van Winkle of a man—a long white beard to match—stepped out of it, an ancient Hawken cradled in his arms.

"Friend or foe?" the man drawled, leveling the rifle.

Longarm pulled his horse to a halt. "Friend."

"Prove it."

"You must be Ike Callahan."

"That's my name, sure enough."

"Jed told me to meet him here."

"He's come and gone."

"Dammit, I told him to wait here for me."

"Well, he didn't. Take care of your horse out back. There's a trough there, grain, and a lean-to. I'll be inside. Yer just in time. Supper's on."

He walked back into the cabin. Whatever the mountain man was cooking smelled good. A moment later, his horse seen to, Longarm entered the cabin.

Ike was bending over something simmering in a huge pot over the fireplace. The savory odor coming from it filled the cabin.

"When did Jed leave?"

"Not long ago. Not more'n an hour."

"What was his hurry?"

"Black Dove." He dropped a handful of pepper into the pot and began to stir it carefully with a long wooden spoon. "She was the one in a hurry. Feller called Tex was after her."

"You mean she was here with Jed?"

Ike nodded.

"Where'd Jed say he was going?"

Ike lifted the wooden spoon to his lips and sipped carefully. "Back to St. Louis."

"St. Louis?"

"Yep." Ike put the spoon aside and stood up. "And before he left, he said the damnedest thing."

"What?"

"Said he wasn't going to read any more Beadle dime novels."

102

Longarm laughed and slacked into a chair by the kitchen table. "What's that you're cookin'? Smells good."

"That, sir, is muskrat stew—an ambrosia fit for the gods."

"It smells like son-of-a-bitch stew."

"My stew has long since graduated from such crude company."

"That so?"

He grinned at Longarm. "I promise you."

Longarm was amused by the man's speech and manner. It was obvious this mountain man was more educated than most. He looked to be as lean and tough as a hickory stick. Despite his age, his eyes were as clear as a babe's and the skin above his beard—tanned chocolate by the sun and wind—was as smooth and flawless as a young woman's. He had a thick shock of snow-white hair to match the long white beard extending from his chin clear to his waist. He was dressed in doeskin leggins and shirt, with knee-high boots of the same material, similar in design to those favored by the Apaches. From where Longarm sat, he could smell the man, the not unpleasant, strong scent of a healthy animal—not that of an unclean human, which Longarm reckoned to be the vilest, most detestable stench of all.

The cabin's back walls were covered with bookshelves, each one crowded with volumes. How the mountain man had managed to lug so many books up to this eagle's nest was a mystery to him. But there they were, and the books looked well-thumbed.

Ike added a pinch of salt to the stew, stirred it in

thoroughly, then left the fireplace and joined Longarm at the table.

Longarm said, "You mentioned Black Dove was running from Tex?"

"Yep," Ike said. "She told me she'd come here because she knew I'd help her. She was a very happy young Flathead squaw when she saw Jed already here with me."

"She didn't happen to mention where Tex might be holed up? Him and the Cheyenne Kid?"

"You after the Kid, are you?"

"That's right."

Ike shook his head in wonderment. "The Cheyenne Kid. An overly romantic, fancy name, wouldn't you say? These killers and thieves. Every man jack of them is a fool romantic—or they wouldn't be out here in the first place."

"That why you're out here?"

He grinned at Longarm. "Precisely. I'm a fool romantic too. That's why I recognize 'em when I see 'em."

"You haven't answered my question, Ike. Did Black Dove say where Cheyenne was holing up?"

"I gathered Cheyenne's got a hideout somewhere outside Timber City."

"Timber City?"

"A logging town over the next ridge. Some loggin's going on still, but not much. There's precious little call today for railroad ties. But it's a good place for outlaws and men on the dodge like Cheyenne to use for purchasing provisions, including booze and women."

Ike sniffed the air abruptly, then got to his feet and hurried over to the fireplace. He took the pot off the tripod and lugged it over to the table. As he planted it down in the center of the table, he cocked an eyebrow at Longarm and asked if he had ever tasted muskrat stew.

"Never have," Longarm admitted.

Ike placed two large bowls down on the table, wooden spoons beside them. Then he ladled the stew into Longarm's bowl and his own.

"How does it smell?"

Longarm took a whiff. The savory odor was enough to make his jaws ache in anticipation.

"Magnificent."

"Eat up then before it cools off."

Ike brought over the coffee and filled his own cup, then pushed the pot over to Longarm. By that time, however, Longarm was too caught up devouring the stew to pour any coffee. Large, surprisingly sweet chunks of muskrat swam in a thick broth alongside potatoes, some tender greens, and wild onions. Ike had not needed to worry about the stew cooling off. The onions took care of that; and as Longarm spooned the stew into his mouth, sweat stood out on his brow. A feeling of deep contentment filled his belly, and an almost miraculous infusion of energy transformed him. Ike had not understated his case. His muskrat stew was indeed an ambrosia fit for the gods.

The huge pot was half empty in a short while, but Longarm was close to bursting and pushed away his bowl when Ike offered him more. Longarm filled his cup with coffee and as he did so, Ike freshened it with Clampett moonshine.

"You won't be getting much more of that tarantula juice from now on," Longarm commented.

"How so?"

Longarm explained to him what he had done to the Clampetts' still, but when he finished, Ike assured him that John Clampett and his crew of moonshiners would be up and producing within a month at most. Clampett had too many willing customers in the towns around. Especially in Timber City.

Ike got up and suggested Longarm move out of the cabin while he cleaned up, waving away Longarm's offer to help.

"I'll be faster and more thorough by myself," he told Longarm. "I'll be right out. Won't take long."

Stepping out onto the cabin's low porch, Longarm found a beat-up wicker chair and a rocker. He slumped into the wicker chair, wishing he was not all out of cheroots. When Ike came out, he brought with him two clay pipes tamped to the brim with tobacco. He handed one to Longarm, then eased his slight frame into the rocker and lit up. Longarm thumb-flicked a wooden match to life and lit the clay pipe. The bite was sharp, but not at all unpleasant.

The two sat without talking for a while, drinking in the vista that opened before them, listening to the birdcalls. Two hawks were drifting high above the timbered peaks.

"You mind telling me," Longarm said abruptly, unable to contain his curiosity any longer, "what a mountain man is doing in this country. The beaver's been trapped out for twenty years now at least."

"More than twenty years, and that's a fact. And no one wears beaver hats anymore. Which means there's no likelihood of my getting rich trapping." He smiled contentedly. "And that's just the way I like it."

"That don't make sense, Ike."

"You got any idea how crowded this country was when mountain men were swarming all over the place, armies of them whoopin' and hollerin', trapping every stream, shootin' grizzlies and buffalo like they were sparrows on a telegraph wire?"

"Sounds grim enough at that."

"Mountain men! With only a few exceptions, a no-account breed. I was determined to outlast them foul-smelling, foul-mouthed children of misfortune—and I did. This here country is mine now. There's no beaver left and precious few buffalo—and the grizzlies no longer cover mountain slopes foraging for berries—but it's a lot quieter and more peaceable. Gives a man time to reflect and contemplate, and that's just the way I like it."

"You got any kinfolks back East?"

"Nope. Not a one."

"Anyone else?"

"You mean do I have a woman back there?"

"I guess that's what I meant."

Ike puffed a moment on his pipe before replying. "You remember that story Washington Irving wrote about Rip Van Winkle?"

"I remember. It was the first thing I thought about when I saw you."

Ike chuckled. "This beard, you mean. Anyway, you remember how this poor fellow went off into the Catskills and took a draft of some queer-tasting moonshine provided by a band of strange little men."

"They were playing kingpins."

"Yep. Anyway, the moonshine put Rip to sleep and

when he woke up it was twenty years later—and he was twenty years older with a beard down to his waist—like mine."

"I remember."

"The point is, when Rip got back to his village, he became a celebrity, and never had to pay for another drink at the local tavern. And his wife was dead and gone. He'd escaped his wife—and her tongue. As Irving put it, a woman's tongue is the only instrument that sharpens with use."

Longarm chuckled.

"I never did forget that description of a woman's tongue. It's the truest thing Irving ever wrote. So Rip escaped his shrew of a wife. It took twenty years out of his life to get rid of her—but it was worth it."

"So what you're doing out here is sleeping for twenty years."

"Precisely. Only I don't intend to go back home when the twenty years are up. That woman of mine—and her razor-sharp tongue—is liable to be waiting for me."

"Nagged you, did she?"

"Do bears defecate in the woods? Longarm, I like to read."

"I noticed the books in your cabin."

"Food and drink to me. But whenever that harridan saw me with a book in my hand, she found something for me to do. She'd say, 'You got nothin' better to do than read them fool books? Why don't you get off your backside and fix the fence?' Or the roof—or the porch. Or something. I don't know what it was, but the sight of me perfectly content with a pipe in my mouth and a book in my hand aroused her to a fury." He shook his head as he remembered.

"So you came West."

"And I haven't once regretted it. Not even when the wind comes straight from the Arctic and the drifts bury this cabin and I have to stay up all night to keep a fire going."

For a moment the two sat in silence while Longarm absorbed Ike's story; then he forced himself to remember what he was doing here in the first place. He stirred himself and leaned forward.

"I just thought of something."

"What's that?"

"If Black Dove was fleeing from Tex, wouldn't you say he'd be due by now?"

"Not necessarily. Black Dove knows this country. I don't think this Texan knows it that well. He could get lost down there. This is big country, and there are no streetlights or railroad tracks. He could be lost forever in that wilderness and no one would ever hear of him again."

"I reckon."

Ike frowned suddenly, then sighed and shook his head.

"What's the matter?"

"Longarm, do you know what the greatest tragedy in the world is?"

"I'll bite."

"It's a beautiful theory killed by a fact."

"What do you mean?"

"Look down there."

Ike pointed to a spot far down the trail. A lone horseman was riding up the slope toward the cabin. Longarm watched the rider closely for a while until he was sure.

Then he leaned back. No question. It was Tex. Ike glanced at Longarm and shook his head sadly.

"So much for my theory," Ike said. "From the look of it, this feller Tex ain't lost, not one bit."

"When he gets here, he's not going to be happy when he finds out Black Dove is gone. You got much more of that muskrat stew?"

"I do. Half a pot."

"Heat it up. That should be enough to pacify him. It sure as hell pacified me."

Ike chuckled, got up from his rocker, and headed for the cabin door. "I'll keep my Hawken handy," he said. "Just in case."

He disappeared into the cabin.

Longarm sat back in his chair and puffed on the clay pipe, wondering if it would help him to quit smoking cheroots if he took up clay pipes instead.

Eventually Tex's hat and then his entire torso astride his horse came into view. When he gained the clearing in front of the cabin and caught sight of Longarm sitting back casually in the wicker chair, puffing on his clay pipe, he pulled his horse to a sudden halt. Longarm waved. Tex studied Longarm for a moment or two, frowning, then urged his horse on across the small flat toward the cabin. A few feet from the porch, he halted and folded his arms over the pommel to gaze in some perplexity at Longarm. Longarm met Tex's perplexed gaze with an amused smile. After a moment, Tex broke the silence.

"Howdy, Longarm."

"Howdy, Tex."

"Last time I saw you, you was under a bed."

"I remember. That stick of dynamite didn't do it.

Except for Len Turco. So now that leaves only you and Cheyenne."

"That was business, Longarm. Nothin' personal."

"That makes me feel a helluva lot better to hear that."

Tex grinned. "I suppose it would at that. How the hell did you get here?"

"It's a long story. Light and set a spell. Ike's inside."

"And Black Dove?"

"Been and gone. Left with Jed Tumbrill. They're probably halfway to St. Louis by now."

"*That's* where he's takin' her?"

Longarm nodded.

"Shit."

"You gonna stay on that horse till nightfall? Light and set a spell."

"I got to keep going. My heart's set on that little Indian lady, and that's a fact. She's all eyes and lips and she sets a man's heart to singing. She ain't no woman for the likes of Jed Tumbrill."

"That may be true. But he's the one has her now— and she's mighty pleased at the prospect."

Tex hesitated a moment, then dismounted.

"There's a lean-to in the back. And some water and grain for the horse."

Tex led his mount past Longarm. As he did so, he sniffed the air. "What's that I smell?"

"Ike's muskrat stew. He's heatin' it up for you."

Tex's blue eyes—still so light as to resemble holes in his head—lit up at the thought. His pace quickened as he led his horse around behind the cabin. Longarm got up from the chair, used a porch post to knock out the contents of his pipe, then went inside the cabin.

• • •

Not long after, Longarm watched Tex gobble up the last of the muskrat stew. Finished, Tex leaned back, wiped his mouth off with the back of his hand, sat back, and patted his tummy.

"Best son-of-a-bitch stew I ever ate," he told Ike, with a quick nod of appreciation.

"Compliments to the cook are always appreciated," Ike said.

Tex glanced over at Longarm. "You still bound and determined to bring Cheyenne and me in?"

"Of course."

"Why? Hell, man, you're way out of your territory. And with Len Turco dead, you ain't got no more federal warrant."

Longarm shrugged. "Sam Calder was a friend of mine."

"Hell, he was a friend of Cheyenne's too."

"Some friend."

"And besides, Cheyenne gave you a chance back there when he took the guns away from them two maggots who was so damned eager to see you shot dead or flung off a cliff. You'd be a dead man now if it weren't for that."

"Makes no difference."

"Is that all you can say?"

"It's all I need to say. You can tell Cheyenne that when you ride back to him."

"You think I'm giving up this easy? I told you already. I'm after that Flathead squaw, and I ain't letting that jackass Jed Tumbrill have her."

"Not even if it's what she wants?" Ike asked Tex.

112

"She ain't had no chance to make a comparison. I guarantee you, I know how to satisfy a savage wench like that."

"Do you now?"

"You're damn right I do."

"Has it ever occurred to you that Black Dove might prefer a gentler, more loving man—someone who will not treat her as a chattel?"

"Chattel?"

"Slave, piece of furniture, something that can be used as a medium of exchange in barter, say, or as collateral to secure a loan."

"What the hell are you talking about?"

"It'll soon be dark," Longarm reminded Tex. "You might as well give up on overtaking her this late."

"I'm only a few hours behind her. They'll have to make camp tonight. I'll find them. Don't you worry none about that."

"We won't," said Ike.

Longarm glanced at Ike, said nothing, then left the table and went outside to watch the sunset. A few minutes later, Ike joined him. When Tex came out after them a few minutes later, a newly built cigarette in his mouth, Longarm brought the barrel of his six-gun down on the top of his head. Tex groaned, his knees buckling. Ike caught him under the arms before he hit the ground.

Chapter 9

They kept Tex on ice for three more days, giving Jed
and Black Dove all the time they would need to make
good their escape to St. Louis. Tex was furious at first
and they had to keep a twenty-four-hour guard on him,
but generous portions of Ike's muskrat stew gradually
wore down his truculence, and when he rode off finally
on his way back to Timber City, Tex was a mite flabby
around the middle, and his disposition had sweetened
noticeably.

When he rode off, Tex waved good-bye to a solitary
Ike, since Longarm had left the night before. He was
standing in a window of the Timberman's Hotel in Timber City when Tex rode in close to sundown. He watched
Tex ride up to the hitch rack in front of the Timber City
Saloon across the street, dismount, and shoulder his way
past the batwings.

Longarm took out a cheroot he had purchased in the
hotel lobby, pulled up a chair, and sat down to wait for

Tex to come out. He would have to come out eventually and ride on to Cheyenne's place.

And when he did, Longarm would follow.

Someone rapped softly on his door.

A frown on his face, he left the window and opened the door a crack to peer out. A girl in a red skirt and white bodice was standing in the hallway. A bright red kerchief held down her thick coils of auburn hair.

"Yes?"

"You wanna woman, mister?" She had a Mexican accent.

"Yeah. A woman. Not a girl."

He started to close the door. She stepped closer to it.

"I am as good as any woman. Try me."

"Some other time."

She pulled down the top of her bodice so he could see the snowy white breasts. "You see? I am a woman already."

"This is a helluva conversation, miss. Ain't you embarrassed, selling your goods door to door?"

"That is a cruel thing to say."

"Well, ain't you?"

"I do not want to be one of the girls in the saloon, or in Ma Torey's whore house. I like to choose the men I go with."

"How come you chose me?"

"I saw you ride in. I say to myself there is a man who could use a woman and who would pay her well. Was I wrong?"

Longarm shook his head and almost closed the door; then, peering at her more closely, he realized that she

116

was older than he had at first thought. Old enough and wise enough, he realized. With a shrug, he pulled open the door and stepped back.

"Come in," he said. "Get out of the cold. Or something."

"Then you want me?"

"I got a long wait. Maybe you can share it with me."

She entered and he closed the door behind her. Brushing past him, she walked over to his bed and folded back the coverlet, punched the pillow, then sat down on the bed and took off her shoes. After she had set them neatly side by side under his bed, she stood up, unsnapped her skirt, stepped out of it, then reached back and pulled off her chemise. Her bloomers came next, and after that there was nothing left to come off. She folded each garment neatly and placed it on top of the dresser. Turning to face him, she untied her red kerchief and shook out her lustrous hair, letting her thick curls tumble down onto her milk-white breasts. Then she stood quietly before him, her dark patch glowing in the dim light, her breasts taut, thrusting, the nipples standing at attention.

"How you like see me strip in front of you like that?"

"It's a real crowd-pleaser. How much this going to cost me?"

"I not haggle. If you a gentleman like you look, you will treat me right."

"What's your name?"

"Donna."

"You got a last name?"

"In this profession, why you want to know more?"

Longarm laughed softly. "I'd say you know your way around for a young lady your age. Just how old are you?"

"Old enough to satisfy a man. You want to shut up now and fuck me?"

"I told you. I got a long wait. I got to stick close to this window. I'm watching for someone."

"Who?"

"The Cheyenne Kid's sidekick. Tex Merrill."

She spat. "He is peeg!"

"Who? Tex or Cheyenne."

"Both. But Tex is more bad than the other one."

"Now, how would you know that?"

"I go to this Cheyenne Kid's place, but Tex took me when the Kid was done."

"You didn't like that?"

"I tol' you. I go to fuck Cheyenne. Not Tex."

"You say you rode out to his place?"

"Yes. I always go to the man. Like here." She put her hands on her hips and tipped her head. "Hey, you really going to stay by that window?"

"Guess I won't have to."

She smiled. "That's better."

"If you know where Cheyenne's hideout is, you've just made things a whole lot easier for me."

"You don' make no sense. Come over here and I will take off your clothes."

"I can handle it," he said.

He started to peel out of his clothes, but she pulled him to her and with swift, practiced fingers had him as naked as a jaybird in a twinkling. Then she pulled him down onto the bed on top of her and spread her

118

legs, arching up at him as she did so. He entered her smoothly, plunging all the way to the bottom. Her gasp became a cry as she tightened around his erection and flung her arms about his neck to squeeze him closer to her. He felt her body go taut as he began his powerful thrusting, going deeper with each massive stroke.

"Ah, yes," Donna whispered hoarsely, her arms still tight around his neck, her breath searing his ear. "This I have waited for so long. A real gentleman! But I have this problem."

"What problem."

"I scream bad when I come!"

"Then don't come."

"You must be crazy."

"So scream," he panted.

"When I scream, you must kiss me hard so I not scream so much."

Longarm nodded and kept right on stroking, building steadily. His lips found hers. Her mouth yawned wide and his darting tongue met hers. He kept up his stroking, driving still deeper, feeling her shudder with each power-ful thrust. Her hands grabbed the hair on the back of his head, holding his lips hard on hers. Longarm continued thrusting into her, feeling her cries surging deep in her throat. And then she was writhing under him wildly, and her lips broke loose from his and she cried out. He was reaching for his own orgasm now, and drove into her with long, hard strokes. He went over the edge just as Donna began to shudder wildly under him. As he expended his seed into her, she let out a sharp, happy yelp.

He trapped her next scream with his lips until the

laxness of her muscles told him that her need to scream had passed. He lifted his face from hers and grinned down at her.

"That was good fuck, hey?" she gasped, sighing deeply.

"It was damn good, as a matter of fact."

"I enjoy my work."

"Seems like it."

"Now maybe I show you few tricks, eh?"

"Hell, woman, you've done wrung me out good and proper."

"A man such as you is like young bull. You are not wrung out, I think."

"Donna?"

"Yes?"

She rested her head on his chest, then let her fingers trace idly down past his hips, then lower, into his crotch. He felt his loins stirring back to life.

"Donna," he said, ignoring her fingers as best he could, "if you've been out to Cheyenne's place, you know how to get there."

"Of course. I tol' you that already."

"Then you can take me out there. Tomorrow, maybe?"

Her hand slowly enclosed his private parts. He swallowed.

"First you tell me why you after Cheyenne."

"He's a wanted man."

"You a lawman?"

"No, I'm a gentleman. Remember?"

"Ah, yes," she said, squeezing him gently. "I remember."

"Will you take me out there?"

"Why should I stick my neck out?"

"You said you didn't like Tex."

"That's right. I don't like Tex. But I don' want to die because I don' like heem."

"You won't die. Just take me out there and point out his place. Then you can ride on back."

"Oh, you are so nice to me. You let me ride back alone all that way. Maybe you are not such a gentleman."

"I need your help, Donna."

She sighed. "All right. I am such a fool for a beeg man like you."

She kissed him on the lips, then moved down his belly, and a moment later her sorcery had brought him back to life with a vengeance. One thing led to another and not long after, Donna had climbed atop Longarm, rocking.

"Mmm. This is so nice," she murmured dreamily. "I think I go on like this forever."

"Not on top of me, you won't."

"Why not?" She pouted.

"Something's happening down there I can't quite control—not much longer anyway."

He reached up and grabbed her hipbones and began slamming her down upon his erection with an enthusiasm that caused her to throw her head back and laugh. She was still laughing when they both came and she collapsed forward onto his chest. He chuckled himself as he stroked her thick hair and regained his breath.

When they'd both rested for a while, Donna turned her head to face his. "This Cheyenne. Is it true what they say? That he have much gold dust?"

"It's true. He rescued it from a Wells Fargo shipment."

"Mmm, so maybe that is why."

"Why what?"

"The Clampetts are going to see Cheyenne."

Fully alert now, Longarm propped himself up on an elbow and looked at her closely. "What's that? The Clampetts? You mean they're in town?"

"*Sí.*"

"Which ones?"

"Will, Ned, and the old man."

"What else can you tell me?"

"About the Clampetts?"

"Yes."

She shrugged. "I not hear very much. Old John Clampett say he mus' rebuild his stills, needs money. When the barkeep across the street and the owner of the hotel wouldn't help him, he was very nasty. He said he would get the money from Cheyenne."

"When was this?"

"This afternoon."

"And where are the Clampetts now?"

"In the hotel, I think."

"Jesus."

"Hey, you know the Clampetts?"

"You might say that."

"Then maybe you let them tell you where Cheyenne's place is. Then I will not have to ride so far."

"It's not as simple as that."

"Why?"

Longarm told her exactly why the Clampetts were in town looking for help in rebuilding their moonshining operation. When he finished, she looked at him closely, obviously trying to picture him causing that much havoc and disruption to the Clampett clan.

"You crazy," she said. "This John Clampett is very mean man. Him and his sons and the men working for him. Maybe you better get out of this hotel."

"If I didn't know he was here, there's a good chance he doesn't know I'm here either. I'll just keep my ass down, and when the three of them move out tomorrow, heading for Cheyenne's place, I'll just follow after them."

"And I can stay here," she said, leaning back with a smile.

"That's right. You won't have to make that long ride after all."

A shout came from the street below. Then another. Booted feet started running. Both Longarm and Donna reached the window at the same time. Longarm snuffed out the lamp so he could see more clearly.

What he saw was Ned Clampett fighting with Tex like two dogs over a bone. A huge, shouting mob was rapidly forming around the two combatants.

"Stay here," Longarm told Donna as he snatched up his trousers and began to dress. "I'm going down there."

"You jus' say you goin' to keep your ass down."

"I changed my mind."

"Then I will not stay here and wait for you."

"Suit yourself."

"But you have not paid me!"

As he slipped into his frock coat, he dug into a pocket and tossed a double eagle at her. She gasped with delight as she caught it with both hands.

With a quick wave, Longarm hurried from the room.

Down in the street Longarm slowly inched his way through the onlookers cheering on the brawling men, until he stood on the inside ring of spectators. He glanced quickly about for John Clampett and Will, and found them standing amidst the townsmen crowding the porch. John Clampett's left arm rested in a sling.

Longarm stepped back out of sight into the crowd.

It looked as if Ned was getting the shit kicked out of him. Twice since Longarm had arrived on the scene, Tex had knocked Ned to the ground, and each time Ned had staggered to his feet, his swings had been wilder and less effective. At the moment he was upright, swaying drunkenly, wiping a streak of blood off his chin. One of Tex's punches had flattened his nose and the resulting flow from it bubbled past his lips.

"Come on," said Tex. "I ain't finished with you yet."

Ned blinked, swayed uncertainly, but said nothing.

"You through then?" Tex demanded. "Had enough?"

Ned didn't have that much sense. Eyes wild, he suddenly put his head down and charged Tex like a demented bull. Tex braced himself, and when Ned piled into him, he grabbed Ned by the shoulders and flung him back, then proceeded to drive him relentlessly backward, clipping him in the face with a right, then a left. A right. A left. Another right. Another left.

The crowd gave before them as Tex drove Ned into their midst. By this time Ned was barely able to paw feebly back at his tormentor. Meanwhile, each punch Tex landed caused the onlookers to cheer, and the brutal, approving shout following each blow seemed to crush Ned even further. Ned suddenly dropped his arms and gave up all efforts to fight back. His face resembling raw hamburger, he sagged to the ground on his knees, then crashed forward. Once he hit, facedown, he did not stir again.

"Pa!" Will cried. "Don't!"

Longarm glanced up to see Old Man Clampett, his eyes wild, leaping from the porch. Before Tex could turn to ward off the blow, Clampett struck Tex viciously on the back of his head with the barrel of his Colt. Tex groaned; his knees sagged. Again Clampett brought up his gun, and it was clear then that he intended to crush Tex's skull with his next blow.

Longarm pushed through the crowd and shoved the barrel of his .44 into Clampett's belly. Clampett flinched and turned his head. When he saw who it was, his face blackened with rage.

"You!" he cried.

"That's right, Clampett. Me. Drop that gun."

"Watch out, mister!" someone called.

As the crowd stampeded away to get out of the line of fire, Longarm turned to see Will aiming his Colt at him from the saloon porch. He flung Clampett to one side and swung up his .44. The two men fired at the same time. But it was Will who folded forward and plunged loosely down the steps.

Clampett uttered an anguished cry and rushed to Will's side. Sobbing, Ned lunged across the ground to his brother. Clampett cradled Will in his arms and began to rock back and forth. It appeared that Will's wound was mortal.

"Get me out of here," Tex told Longarm, grimacing painfully as he clung to Longarm. "My head's hurt bad."

Longarm holstered his Colt and guided Tex through the crowd and across the street to the hotel. Inside, he helped Tex up the stairs to his room. When he pushed open the door, he found Donna dressed and waiting. Longarm kicked the door shut as Donna hurried over and helped Longarm get Tex to the bed. When Tex reached it, he collapsed forward onto the bed, out cold.

"I watch from the window," Donna told Longarm. "I see what that monster Clampett do to Tex. Tex lucky he not crack open his skull."

"He's going to have a headache for sure," Longarm said, frowning down at the unconscious outlaw. "That was a mean crack he took."

Donna took off Tex's hat and shuddered as she gazed down at the bloody gash on his head. She looked up at Longarm. "You do not mind if I help?"

"I thought you didn't like Tex."

She looked back down at the man. "I admit, this one did take me when I not want him to—but when he finish, he was very generous. He give me much gold dust."

"And that made it all right, eh?"

She shrugged.

Tex groaned and stirred to life. "My head," he muttered. "It's busted."

"You got a bad gash there, Tex," said Longarm. "But that thick head of yours ain't broke."

"That ain't no comfort."

"You mind telling me why you and Ned were battling like that?"

126

"Sure. He was picking on the saloon's swamper. Wouldn't let up on the poor son of a bitch. I took offense, stepped between him and Ned."

"A swamper?"

"They're human too, Longarm. Hell, any one of us could end up in some saloon at the end of our days, working for booze and whatever we find in the sawdust."

"Speak for yourself," Longarm said with a shudder. "Not me."

"How do you feel?" Donna asked Tex, leaning close.

Tex smiled grimly at her. "Like someone drove a railroad spike through my fool head. You still mad at me, Donna?"

"No more," she said.

"Donna," Longarm said. "Can you get some water and towels?"

"*Sí.*"

She hurried from the room.

Longarm became aware of a growing commotion in the street below. He went to the window and looked down. The crowd in front of the saloon had grown. Will's body was no longer sprawled at the bottom of the saloon's steps. Longarm looked carefully but could not see Old Man Clampett or Ned. He noticed then that most of the men running up to join the crowd were lugging rifles and shotguns.

It had the look and sound of a lynch crowd.

Donna returned carrying a basin, two towels draped over her outstretched arms.

"Longarm," she told him as she put the pan of water down on the night table beside Tex. "I hear the men talking downstairs in the lobby. So I sneak down the stairs to listen. Will Clampett is dead and the old man and his son are raising a posse to come after you."

"That's no surprise," Longarm said, walking over to the bed. "I been watching that necktie party gathering in front of the saloon."

"Clampett threaten the saloon owner and the one who own thees hotel.

"He say there will be no moonshine—or any other liquor—for thees town if they do not string up you and Tex. And beside that, he offer big reward for one who bring you down."

Longarm cocked an eyebrow. "How much?"

"A hundred dollar."

"Where the hell's the town marshal?"

She frowned. "You must be crazy. There is no law in thees town. It is wide open. How you not know this?"

"Sorry I asked."

"We must hurry. They know what room you are in."

"Bind up Tex's head," he told her. "Then get the hell out of here."

"I think I stay with you."

"Damnit, Donna. Why?"

"If we help Tex escape, he will share more of his gold dust with me. He is very generous."

"And very foolish. Besides, that gold dust is not his to share. It belongs to Wells Fargo."

"Are you a Pinkerton maybe?"

"Never mind that. See to Tex."

She dabbed at the gash, cleaned it out, then wrapped a fresh towel around his head. Tex sat up, holding his head gingerly.

"You ready for travel?" Longarm asked him.

"My head's cracked open, I'm telling you."

"See if you can you stand up."

"I'm seein' double, for Christ's sake."

"The thing is, Tex, Clampett and half the town will be up here in a few minutes to tear our heads off."

"Guess maybe I can stand up," Tex muttered.

He eased himself upright and clapped his hat back on, grimacing as he did so. Because of the towel, the hat rode high on his head, but it was snug enough. Longarm gathered up his gear and led Tex, still unsteady, out of the door and down the hallway to the back stairs.

The three of them were a few steps from the door leading out to the alley when it burst open and two men charged in. They were armed with shotguns, and when Longarm saw the yawning bores, he kicked the shotgun out of the grasp of the nearest townsman. The shotgun landed hard and detonated, expending its charge into the ceiling. Longarm slammed the other man against the wall and clubbed him to the floor. Then he pushed through the door into the alley, Tex and Donna close behind him.

Shouting men were running down the alley toward them.

"This way!" Donna cried.

She darted straight across the alley past a privy, kept going, and came out on a narrow back street, Longarm and Tex following. The need to save his neck was giving Tex a real incentive to keep up with them. They kept on down the street, found another side street, turned onto it. Halfway down the street, they came to a small white clapboard house, a neat white picket fence enclosing its

129

front yard. Donna led them through the gate and around to the rear of the house, where she mounted a small porch and knocked insistently on the back door. In a few minutes it was flung open and a round, apple-cheeked woman in her fifties, a lighted lamp held high, peered out at them.

"Millie," Donna cried. "You got to hide us!"

"What've you done?"

"She ain't done nothin'," Tex told her. "But I'm hurt bad and there's a howlin' mob after us."

"That you, Tex?"

"Yeah."

"Who's that with you?"

"A friend."

"All right." She blew out the lamp. "Come in."

Millie kept the house dark. Longarm, crouching by the sitting room window, watched as a knot of townsmen—many carrying torches and all carrying weapons—pounded down the street past the house. Clampett's one-hundred-dollar reward had sure as hell aroused the townsmen.

When the crowd had vanished, Millie lit a lamp on the piano, but kept it burning low. Longarm left the widow. Tex was on the couch, Donna crouched beside him, unwinding the towel she had wrapped around his head.

Millie stood over them, watching.

"Nice place you got here, Millie," Longarm told her.

"Best whore house in the territory until I closed it," she said. "And Donna was my best girl."

"She told me she didn't like working in parlor houses."

"She don't. I didn't run my place like most parlor

130

houses. She's doin' what I told her, running her own business and picking her own gentlemen friends."

"Millie," said Donna, "come look at this, will you?"

Millie left Longarm and bent over Donna's shoulder to peer at the gash in Tex's skull. Muttering something about getting some carbolic acid and water, Millie hurried from the sitting room.

Longarm slumped in a chair, beside which he had dumped his bedroll and saddlebags. As he watched Donna fussing over Tex, he wondered how in the hell he had managed to become Tex's guardian angel. He could have melted back into the crowd and let Clampett club him into the ground. But he hadn't done that and he found it difficult to feel any regret for having stepped forward as he had. He told himself that it was because he needed Tex to lead him to the Cheyenne Kid—the outlaw who had killed Sam Calder. Only it wasn't as simple as that. Donna could have led him to Cheyenne's place. No. The truth of it was he just couldn't stand by and watch a cockroach like Clampett kill any man for standing up to one of his sons. Or maybe it was just because he and Tex had enjoyed all that muskrat stew together.

Which was as good an explanation as any other.

Millie returned with a pan containing a strong, acrid-smelling mixture of carbolic acid and water, left, and returned a moment later with fresh bandages. After she returned, the two women worked over Tex for a quiet, intense interval. Throughout, Tex did not stir once. He was out completely. At length, Millie picked up the pan and left the room, leaving Donna to finish bandaging Tex's head. When Millie returned, she walked over to Longarm.

"I want you and Tex out of here before sunup," she told him. "Otherwise, it'll be the end for me here—and this place is all I've got left."

"Sure, Millie. You've already done more than enough. We'll leave as soon as Tex can travel."

"He can't travel. Not on foot."

"My mount is in the livery stable. I'll go after it. Maybe I'll pick up a horse for Tex too."

"Won't that be dangerous?"

"What choice do I have?"

Looking up from Tex, Donna said, "I will go with you."

Longarm got up and walked over to the sofa and looked down at Tex. His eyes were closed and he was breathing regularly, but his face was very pale, Beads of sweat stood out on his forehead. Clampett's blow had been a terrible one, Longarm realized, perhaps with far more deadly effect than either Tex or Longarm had realized at the time. He drew back from Tex and glanced at Donna.

"You think you can handle it?"

"Try me and see."

"I already done that, and you did fine."

She smiled, pleased.

"Let's go then. The sooner we get the horses, the sooner we can ride out of here."

"There's just one thing," Millie said.

"What's that?"

"If you leave that stable with a crowd on your heels, don't come back here. I'll meet you at the door with a loaded shotgun. I told you. I can't afford to be unwelcome in this town."

"You already made your point, Millie," Longarm told her as he headed for the kitchen door with Donna.

The stable owner was nowhere in sight as Longarm and Donna slipped into the livery stable. They could hear the shouts coming from the street in front of the stable and the constant pound of horses' hooves as men rode back to the saloon. Longarm thought he could hear Clampett railing at those who returned empty-handed.

Longarm figured the hostler was out looking for them as well.

The horse barn was alive with the stamping of restless hooves and the smell of straw, horse manure, and piss pounded into the stable floor. Longarm had no difficulty picking out his black. He went right to it with his bedroll, while Donna found her own sorrel and began saddling it. When they finished saddling their mounts, they led them out of their stalls and paused.

"I don't see Tex's horse," said Longarm.

"It's maybe still in front of the saloon."

"Yeah. That's where it is, all right. I saw him leave it at the hitch rack."

Longarm moved to the livery stable's open doors and peered out cautiously. Men were standing around with flickering, guttering torches, and in their flickering light Longarm saw Tex's chestnut, saddled and heavy with gear, its tail drooping as it waited in front of the hitch rack.

On the saloon porch, less than ten feet from the mount, Clampett and Ned were standing. Ned's face was partially bandaged and looked terrible even from this distance. Clampett and Ned were flanked by two older men, one of

133

whom had a huge gut and was wearing an old-fashioned beaver hat. The second one was smaller and more furtive in appearance. A sizable crowd still milled in front of the saloon.

Donna slipped up behind him.

"Who're those two standing with Clampett?" Longarm asked her.

"The one with the beaver hat is Ross Finley, the owner of the lumber mill. He is a pig. The other one owns the feed store. He is a worm."

"Pigs and worms, eh? You know them?"

"I do."

"What about Clampett and his boy Ned. Do you know them too?"

"You forget," she reminded him patiently, "most healthy men around here know me."

"Then it looks like we're not going to get Tex's horse."

"You ride out the back of the barn on your mount and lead my sorrel out behind you," she told him. "I will get Tex's horse."

"You must be crazy."

"Clampett does not know I am with you."

"You can't take that chance," Longarm insisted. "There's plenty more horses in here we can take instead."

"You mean steal one for Tex?"

"Yes."

"So now you are horse thief, eh?"

"We got to get Tex out of town."

"I will wait until you ride out from barn. We meet behind Millie's house. Make sure Tex is ready."

Reluctantly, Longarm mounted up and led her horse toward the rear of the barn.

Donna watched Longarm duck his head and ride out, her sorrel vanishing after him. Then she left the livery and walked down the street past the knots of men still clustered in the street and on the sidewalk. She greeted more than a few by name, and these men doffed their hats in turn. These tough loggers remembered her skilled ministrations and were grateful; after all, it wasn't just any boot-stamper in Timber City who could boast of a visit from Donna. When she reached the saloon, she left the wooden sidewalk and lifted the reins of Tex's chestnut off the hitch rack. In one quick bound she was astride the horse, reining it back into the street.

"Hey, there, young lady," roared Clampett, his lean, hawklike face dark with suppressed fury. "Where you goin'? That ain't your hoss."

"That's right," said Ross Finley. "What're you up to, girl?"

The crowd surged quickly around Donna, the men grinning up at her, waiting eagerly for her response.

"Why, Mr. Finley," Donna said. "You mean you don't know my business?"

A roar erupted from the crowd. The night was getting long in the tooth, and these men welcomed this diversion.

"Now, come, come," said Finley. "Ain't it a bit late for that, young lady?"

"Maybe for a walrus like you. But not for the young man I got in mind."

The crowd whooped and applauded.

"You're stealin' someone's hoss," Clampett reminded

her, his eyes wild with frustration at this night's murderous business. "And horse stealin's a hangin' offense." He seemed eager to shed *someone's* blood, even Donna's, if it could satisfy his lust for vengeance.

"You silly man," she retorted airily. "You mean you don' know who this horse belongs to?"

"Hey, that's right, Clampett," someone in the crowd sang out. "That's Tex's chestnut!"

"You see?" said Donna, smiling sweetly at Clampett. "I figure Tex won't be needing it no more. That hundred-dollar reward should bring him and that other one in soon. Ain't that right, Mr. Clampett?"

"You're damn right, it is," the man growled. "Them two sons of bitches won't last the night."

"I can take his horse then?"

"Take it, whore," Clampett snarled, "and welcome to it."

The crowd cheered.

"Good night, gentlemen," Donna called to the townsmen crowding close about her. "Maybe soon I visit the lucky man who gets that beeg reward!"

With a wave, she turned the horse and rode off down the street. When the men stopped cheering, they watched her vanish into the night with hungry looks in their eyes.

Chapter 10

Tex had difficulty staying on the chestnut, and Longarm had to ride close alongside to steady him. At dawn they halted. As Donna pulled Tex from his saddle, he suddenly broke away from her and ran off, babbling crazily. They caught up to him finally well after sunup. Still babbling, Tex was standing hip deep in a mountain stream. He didn't seem to know who they were, and by the time they got him back to the horses he was shivering violently.

They made camp by the stream, built a fire, and wrapped Tex in blankets to warm him up. They managed to stop his shivering, but nothing, it seemed, could stop his wild talk. He was completely out of his head, and Longarm didn't like it. But he was even more concerned when Tex's babbling stopped and he lapsed into unconsciousness.

"How much farther is it to Cheyenne's place?" Longarm asked Donna.

She was pulling a blanket up around Tex's neck. Glancing at him, she said, "I am not sure. I theenk it will take until noon." She pointed to a low pass in the distance. "It is not far beyond that pass."

"I'll stay here with Tex. You go ride to Cheyenne for help."

Donna rested her palm on Tex's forehead, then nodded. "Yes. I theenk that will be best. I go now."

As soon as she had ridden off, Longarm decided that his present camp left him too exposed. He draped Tex over the chestnut's saddle and moved out on foot, leading the two horses. He was not too far from the pass when he spotted a patch of rock outcropping on a sheer above the timberline. He was certain that from such a vantage point he would be able to see Donna returning with Cheyenne.

He turned off the trail and threaded his way up through the timber. It was still early in the day when he reached the rock face and found what he had been hoping to find—the entrance to a cavern, a sheer wall of rock overhanging it.

He lugged Tex into the cave, unsaddled their horses, and dumped their gear in a corner. Then he led the horses into a pine grove hugging the base of the cliff a safe distance from the cavern. Assuring himself that there was enough moisture seeping through cracks in the rock face to slake their thirst and plenty of grass to crop, he tethered the two mounts and returned to the cavern.

Clambering into it once more, he looked about him and figured he had found a pretty damn good redoubt in the unlikely event Clampett and his posse were lucky enough to find his tracks and follow them.

He bedded Tex down in a snug corner of the cavern, then looked the man over. He was still mumbling softly to himself, but outside of that he was reasonably quiet. Longarm piled the saddlebags and bedrolls near the cavern entrance as a cushion, and gazing down at the trail he had left and the forested slopes beyond, he took out a cheroot, lit up, and with a weary sigh leaned back against the saddlebags.

At once he sat up, turned, and swiftly pulled the top saddlebag around onto his lap. It belonged to Tex. He opened it and stuck his hand in.

And froze.

He had just leaned himself back against at least a half-dozen sticks of dynamite. And he hadn't been any too gentle about it either. He studied the sticks of dynamite carefully. Fuses were already implanted in them, coiling like pigs' tails out of each end. All it would take to detonate a stick was a match to light the fuse— or a well-aimed bullet. Either way, the effect would be noticeable. Tex must have taken this dynamite from Len Turco's stash, Longarm realized, when he rode out with Cheyenne. The usefulness of such explosive power had not been lost on Tex.

And it wasn't lost on Longarm now.

He selected three sticks, placed them down beside him with great care, then placed the remainder of the dynamite back into the saddlebag. Very carefully he placed the saddlebag to one side. Only then did he lean back once more against what remained of the cushion he had fashioned. Puffing on his cheroot, he turned his attention to the slope below and the dim trace leading from the pass. He wondered idly if he would ever see Donna or Cheyenne again.

"What's going on, Longarm?"

Startled, Longarm turned to see Tex sitting up, holding his head in both hands and staring bleakly at Longarm.

"I'm waiting for Donna to bring Cheyenne."

"Where the hell are we?"

"Somewhere between Timber City and Cheyenne's place."

"My head hurts real bad."

"Glad you can talk. You been out of your head for quite a while."

"Yeah? What are you doin' with that dynamite?"

"Keeping it handy."

"I'm having trouble seeing. It's daylight, ain't it?"

"Noon, I figure."

"Well, for me it's like the sun keeps going behind a cloud. It's this crack on my head. That sonofabitch Clampett damn near blinded me."

"Well, just stay quiet. We'll get you help."

"Yeah. Sure."

Longarm watched Tex lay back down, his eyes open, a troubled frown on his face. Tex was right. Clampett's vicious blow to his head was undoubtedly the reason he was having difficulty seeing clearly. A few moments later Tex appeared to doze off.

Longarm turned back around and looked down the slope, hoping to hell his misgivings were unfounded and that Donna would be showing up with Cheyenne soon. Squinting in the sun's harsh glare, he tried to keep his eyes on the trail, but it had been a long night and before long, he dozed off—to awake suddenly, his hand reaching out for his rifle.

There was movement in the timber below him. He peered into the trees, but saw nothing. Then came dim shouts, each one closer. This was not Donna returning with the Cheyenne Kid. He was pretty damn sure it was members of Clampett's posse following his tracks. They were making a noisy job of it, but with their numbers they didn't see much need for stealth.

Longarm pulled his Winchester around and jacked a fresh round into the firing chamber, then lay flat and peered down the slope, waiting for the first posse member to emerge from the timber.

He didn't have long to wait. A miner in heavy boots and wearing a red stocking cap emerged into full view pulling his mount after him while he kept his eyes on the ground. Abruptly, he pulled up and looked back down into the timber.

"Up here," he cried.

Two more, then a third and a fourth posse member came into view, all of them pulling their mounts up the steep ground after them. Longarm waited, sighting on the closest. He was hoping to see Clampett step into view, and cursed softly when he did not appear. The first tracker was pointing directly at the rocks now.

"He's up there in that cave, I'm bettin'!"

Longarm dropped his gun sight, and aiming at a spot in front of the man's boots, squeezed off a shot. The ground at the tracker's feet exploded as the Winchester's sharp crack echoed over the slope. With a cry, the man spun about and charged back down the slope, the rest charging after him. In a moment they had disappeared back into the timber, so panic-stricken they had left their mounts behind.

Seizing the opportunity, Longarm sent a steady volley at the feet of the milling horses and soon drove them off at a hard gallop. From the timber then came a steady stream of rifle fire as the entrance to the cave sang with the whine of ricocheting bullets. Longarm kept his head down, sourly aware that if Cheyenne were on his way, the sound of this gunfire would warn him and be sure to keep him from coming any closer.

Which meant it was all Longarm's play from here on.

He put a steady volley into the timber to keep the posse members honest. He had no qualms firing at the men. He knew damn well that they were answering to Clampett, who was after Longarm as well as Tex. When and if he ran out of ammunition and those bastards rushed him, the dynamite sitting on the ground beside him would blow at least some of the bastards to kingdom come. It was not much, perhaps, but it was all he had, and would sure as hell take the vinegar out of this posse.

At last Clampett showed.

The familiar rake handle of a figure emerged from the timber and stood calmly, arrogantly, in full view, shading his eyes as he peered up at the cavern's entrance. Longarm could understand the old reprobate's anguish at the loss of two of his sons and the cold fury that had caused him to bankroll this posse, but the moonshiner had brought those awesome losses on himself.

Carefully—very carefully—Longarm took aim on Clampett.

A shattering cry erupted from behind Longarm. He whirled to see Tex, a wild, mad light in his eye, snatch

142

up the three dynamite sticks, shove them down into the front of his shirt, then rush past Longarm and plunge down the slope toward Clampett. As he plowed down the steep slope, he screamed furiously at the old moonshiner, filling the air with his invective. For a moment Clampett was stunned by the sight of this madman tearing down the slope toward him. But he recovered quickly and from where Longarm watched, he could see clearly the mean smile that lit Clampett's face as he drew his Colt and aimed point-blank at the charging Texan. The gun pulsed in his hand.

It was a good clean shot.

The instant the round struck Tex's chest both Tex and Clampett went up in a titanic blast. The mountainside rocked. Debris shot into the air, and for a moment Longarm could see nothing but dust boiling. When the air cleared, all that remained of the two men was a hole in the slope big enough to hold a beer wagon. Except for a distant, persistent echo, an awesome silence fell over the slope. Off in the distance above the trees, swarms of alarmed crows and blackbirds wheeled skyward.

Slowly Longarm got to his feet, rifle at the ready, and waited for members of the posse to show. Gradually, one by one, they left the timber and approached the crater left by the three sticks of dynamite.

"Hey, you down there!" Longarm cried.

Confused and uncertain without their paymaster and leader, the men stopped warily at sight of Longarm. A few ducked back into the timber. Those posse members who remained did not fling up the weapons to get off a shot, and that, Longarm figured, was a good sign.

"What d'you want?" a burly fellow in a red stocking cap called up to Longarm.

"I want to talk."

"Then talk."

"It's over. Clampett is gone and so is Tex. And you don't want me."

"What makes you so sure."

"Tangle with me and you'll be messing with federal law."

"What's that?"

"I'm a federal marshal. It's the Cheyenne Kid I'm after, not any of you. Take me out and you'll have a passel of federal marshals to deal with. And besides, with Clampett dead, you won't get a red cent for your trouble."

The men moved close together to debate the issue. The debate was a short one.

"All right," said the one in the stocking cap. "Which way did our horses go?"

Longarm pointed.

Without another glance up at him, the men started off down the slope after their mounts. Longarm watched them go, then sat back down, took out a cheroot, and lit up. He would wait and see how the wind blew. He didn't trust a single one of them.

He had almost finished the cheroot when Donna stepped out of the timber and stared up at him.

"Longarm!" she called. "Is that you?"

"It's me, all right," he called down to her, getting to his feet. "Where's Cheyenne."

"He did not come. Where is Tex?"

"Wait there. I'll be right down."

He left the cavern carrying his gear with him—including the saddlebag containing the dynamite—and joined Donna on the steep slope. She was nervous, he noted, very nervous.

"My horse is over here in the pines," Longarm told her. "Where's your mount?"

"He . . . broke a leg."

It was a lie. Of that, Longarm was almost certain.

"Well, you're in luck then," he told her. "Tex's chestnut is tethered with mine. You can use his."

"You not yet tell me what happen to Tex."

"I been trying to find the best way to explain it."

"Did I hear big explosion?" she asked, prompting him.

"You did. And that explosion was the end of things for Tex—and for John Clampett."

"What you mean?"

"Tex stuck three sticks of dynamite into his shirt and let Clampett shoot him. Both men went up."

By then, they were in the pines. Longarm dropped his saddle beside the black, went back to the cave for Tex's saddle, then saddled both horses. Just before they mounted up, Longarm took Donna's arm and turned her around sharply to face him.

"What I want to know, Donna, is how that posse knew Tex and I were nearby. How did they know we headed in this direction?"

She looked away from his accusing eyes. "Cheyenne," she said. "It was Cheyenne. He made me tell Clampett."

"Where is Cheyenne now?"

"Right behind you, Longarm."

Longarm spun. Cheyenne was grinning, his six-gun in

his hand, the bore yawning up at Longarm.

"Donna's been a good girl," Cheyenne told him. "Don't blame her. I didn't give her any choice in the matter. That's too bad about Tex. I heard the explosion. If I was on the moon, I would've heard it. It sure must've been one spectacular way to go."

"Think you'd like that, do you?"

"What I'd like is to be rid of you, Longarm."

"You'll have to kill me to do that."

"Just what I was thinking."

"You can't do it. Not with Donna here as a witness."

"I know that. But who says Donna has to stay around?"

"What you mean?" she demanded.

Without answering her, Cheyenne lifted Longarm's Colt from his holster and tossed it into the bushes. Then he deftly removed the derringer from Longarm's watch-fob pocket, dumped its load onto the ground, then dropped the derringer back into the vest's pocket. Then he stepped back to give himself room and clubbed Longarm on the side of the head. Longarm staggered back, then sat down heavily, his head spinning.

Cheyenne turned his attention to Donna then.

One mean swipe of his six-gun sent her rocking back against Tex's chestnut. Cheyenne flung her up into the saddle, slammed her forward, and with her face buried in the mane, took some rope and tied her wrists together under the horse's neck. Then he roped her ankles together under the horse—and with a sudden, sharp crack, slapped the chestnut's rump, sending it crashing out of the pines and down the slope.

Cheyenne turned and grinned down at Longarm.

"See? No witnesses."

"You son of a bitch."

Cheyenne slapped Longarm's mount on the rear and sent him down the slope after the chestnut. Then he swiftly built a hangman's noose in the length of rope he had left and tossed the other end over a branch. He fit the noose over Longarm's head, tightened it, and hauled Longarm brutally erect. Longarm's skull was still ringing from the earlier blow, but he could see clearly enough to know what Cheyenne intended.

"Thing is," said Cheyenne conversationally, as he moved behind Longarm to lash his wrists together, "I ain't no man to shoot anyone in cold blood. It goes against my nature."

"It's all right to shoot them otherwise."

"Sure. In the heat of action—say a train or a bank robbery. That's when a man has to do what has to be done."

"Like shooting Sam Calder in the gut."

Stepping back around in front of Longarm, Cheyenne shrugged. "Such things happen, Longarm. You ought to know that. Sure as hell Sam Calder knew it could happen when he pinned on that tin badge."

"So you won't shoot me. You're going to hang me instead."

"You catch on fast," Cheyenne said approvingly.

He hauled back on the rope and kept tugging on it until Longarm was standing on tiptoes. Then he left Longarm in that position and wrapped the other end of the rope around the trunk of the tree and stepped back to survey his handiwork.

147

"No need for me to be on hand when your ankles get tired," he told Longarm, "or you get tired and slump forward down this slope."

"You bastard," Longarm told him through clenched teeth.

"Yeah. There's no question about that. I really am, you know. A bastard, I mean. Anyway, this time you won't be showing up on my trail later on," he said, pleased, "cutting away my men like you did. You know, I really was surprised when you showed up. I never thought you'd get the better of them two bloodthirsty rascals."

"I might show up again."

Cheyenne grinned. "As a ghost maybe. This is good-bye, lawman. Next time we meet, it'll be in hell."

"Don't bet on it."

"Bluster all you want," Cheyenne said, stepping backward through the pines, "if it makes you feel any better."

And then he was gone.

Chapter 11

Ike Callahan was trying to find the Cheyenne Kid's hideout. All that talk of gold dust had made him consider how easy it would be for him to lift some of it and maybe take a trip back East, visit with a few old friends.

Maybe even find himself a woman.

After all, money talked.

He'd seen the wilderness. He'd read all the books he could find. But it wasn't enough, not nearly enough—if you were always alone and had no one to share your life with. Nothing was worthwhile, truly, until it was shared with someone you loved.

Even with someone you hated.

Suddenly Ike pulled his horse to a halt and squinted down through the trees. A woman on a chestnut had shown for a moment, then vanished from sight. In the brief glimpse he'd had, he'd seen she was riding with her face buried in the horse's mane and part of her was hanging off the horse as it galloped wildly through the timber. It didn't look natural. It looked as if she was tied on. And then he knew that that had to be the truth of it. The woman had been tied onto the horse's back and was about ready to fall off. She could get killed if the horse dragged her any distance.

Ike spurred off the trace he had been following and cut into the timber and, making as good time as he could, rode after the horse and rider. After a long, hard gallop through treacherous woodland, he was about to give up when he saw the chestnut ahead of him in a small clearing, cropping the grass at his feet. The woman's crumpled form was on the ground beside it.

He rode up to the horse and dismounted, recognizing Donna instantly. She had been kind enough to visit him on occasion, willing to accept a book of poems or a novel as payment. She was unconscious, and he could see how cruelly her wild ride had mauled her. The back of her riding jacket was torn and livid scratches crisscrossed her exposed limbs and the back of her neck. When she had fallen off the horse, she had slipped forward over its neck so that her arms, the wrists still bound, were now free. But her legs were still attached to the horse, the rope binding her ankles looped over the saddle, her feet in the air.

Falling in such an awkward way, her back possibly twisting violently out of shape as she landed, she could easily have injured herself severely, Ike realized. Swiftly he untied her ankles and let her legs rest out straight on the grass. The chestnut, free of its awkward burden, glanced back at Ike, flicked its ears, then moved off to crop fresher grass.

Ike untied Donna's wrists and looked around to see if there might be a cool stream nearby. But he saw no sign of any. He took his canteen off his saddlehorn, emptied some water out onto his kerchief, and patted the girl's face and forehead with the damp kerchief.

She opened her eyes, then frowned up at him in astonishment.

"Ike?"

He nodded.

She felt the grass with her opened palms and looked down at her limbs now resting on the grass.

"Thank God," she breathed. "You cut me loose, Ike."

"That must've been some ride."

"It was awful! I thought I was going to die."

"How's your back?"

Slowly, carefully, she bent forward to a sitting position, her hands reaching behind her to feel her back. Satisfied she was all right, she smiled up at Ike.

"I hurt all over, Ike, but I don' think nothin's broke."

Ike winced at her mutilation of spoken English, but said nothing, as pleased as he was to find her not seriously injured.

"Who did this to you?" he asked.

"Cheyenne!" she spat.

"My God, why?"

"He not want me to witness him when he kill Longarm."

"Longarm?"

"Yes."

"You say he's killed Longarm?"

"I think maybe. Yes."

"Where did all this take place?"

She pointed up the steep timbered slope at the massive white outcropping of rock hanging in the air high over it.

"Up there!"

"I can't believe Longarm is dead," Ike said.

Donna shrugged. "Maybe he still lives," she said hopefully. "I do not see Cheyenne kill him."

"Can you ride?"

"I will try."

She got up awkwardly and brushed herself off, then walked gingerly over to the grazing chestnut. She took the hanging reins, dropped them over the horse's neck, and stepped up into the saddle. The horse tossed its head nervously, but she quieted it down with soft words and a firm hand on the reins.

"Yes," she said, looking down at Ike. "I can ride."

"Then lead the way," he said, swinging aboard his own mount.

Longarm did not dare believe his eyes. On a trail far below him appeared riders. The first was Donna, the other Ike Callahan, the old mountain man's long beard flung back over his shoulder like a snow white scarf. They hadn't caught sight of him yet, hidden as he was inside the pines; the only thing now was, could he hold out long enough for them to reach him?

For the past hour or so tiny pebbles had been slipping out from under the toes of his stovepipes. His ankles ached as they had never ached before in his life, while the tendons in the back of his legs were crying out shrilly for relief. But somehow he had managed to keep himself balanced on his toes, staring down a slope that began less

152

than a foot from his toes. It was a slope carpeted with pine needles, and once a single boot came down on that slippery carpet, his feet would fly out from under him, the noose would tighten around his gullet, and he would be launched into oblivion.

It was an outcome he did not envision with any degree of enthusiasm.

When Donna and Ike got closer, he managed a strangled cry that went completely unnoticed. He waited for a short, desperate while and tried again, putting so much into the effort he almost lost his balance. Beads of cold sweat stood out on his brow as he waited patiently a good five minutes or so before trying again. This time his strangled cry reached them. They pulled their horses to a halt and peered into the pines, seemingly right at him.

Again Longarm called out.

This time they caught sight of him. Dismounting quickly, they ran into the pines and up the slope toward him. Ike flung his arms around Longarm's waist to hold him in place.

"Quick, Donna," he told her. "Lift off that noose."

With trembling hands, Donna loosened the noose and lifted it over Longarm's head. He took a deep, grateful breath and stood unaided, the ache in his tendons still excruciating, but fading fast. Ike moved back as Donna hurried behind Longarm and untied his wrists. The two stepped back then to view Longarm, obviously greatly pleased to have arrived when they had. Longarm was even more pleased.

"What the hell kept you?" he asked with a lopsided grin, his voice scratchy from the weight of the noose on his windpipe.

"That was a terrible fix you were in," said Ike, shaking his head. "It took a diabolical mind to conceive such a demise."

"And Cheyenne has such a mind."

"I tell you, he is a devil, that one," said Donna.

"Where is he?" Ike asked.

"Gone back to his place, I think."

Ike turned to Donna. "Maybe you better go back to Timber City," he told her, "and let us tend to Cheyenne."

"You goin' after heem?"

"We are," said Longarm.

"Not without me, you ain't. I am only one who knows way."

"Be reasonable, Donna," said Longarm.

"Hey! He tie me to that horse. He try to kill me too. An' if he not make me tell Clampett where to find Tex, maybe Tex be alive now."

"Not really. Clampett's blow to the head had already done in Tex. He was clean out of his mind."

"I don' care what you say. I go with you two."

Longarm shrugged and looked at Ike. Ike grinned suddenly at Donna.

"Okay," Ike said. "You win. Now all we need is a horse for Longarm."

"It's down there in the timber somewhere," Longarm said, "Cheyenne sent it down there with a whack on its backside."

"Let's go fin' heem," said Donna.

Before they set out, Longarm retrieved his gun from the bushes where Cheyenne had flung it, then reloaded his derringer and set off down through the timber. When they came upon the black finally, Longarm checked the saddlebags, one in particular, and found everything in order. He mounted up, and with Donna leading the way, they arrived at Cheyenne's place late that afternoon. Longarm was pleased to see wood smoke coiling out of the cabin's fieldstone chimney. Cheyenne was inside.

Longarm dismounted, and walked with Ike and Donna to the edge of the ridge and gazed down at Cheyenne's cabin. It sat on a high ledge on the other side of a steep-sided ravine. The cabin was certainly big enough, twice the size and length of the typical log structure, containing at least five or six rooms, judging from the number of windows. The back of it was built snug against the towering cliff wall behind it. This meant that the only approach was from the front, along a narrow trail leading steeply up from the ravine below.

"That's some place he's got," Longarm commented.

"A fortress, pure and simple," Ike said. "Take an army to rout him out of there."

Longarm nodded. Approaching the cabin frontally would be suicide, and there was no other way up to it that Longarm could see.

"We can wait until he moves out," suggested Ike.

"When that be?" Donna asked, not happy with the idea.

"I don't know."

"It better be soon," Longarm said. "If we wait until dark, he might get wind of us and move out. We could lose him."

Even as they watched they saw Cheyenne's tiny figure emerge from the cabin and walk across the lot to his small horse barn. A moment later he emerged with two packhorses and began loading them up. He seemed to be in no particular hurry, but there was no doubt he would be riding out soon.

"You're right," sighed Ike. "He's pullin' out."

"Then we mus' get him now," hissed Donna.

"Yeah," said Ike. "But how? We open up on him, and he'll just duck back into the cabin and wait for dark before pulling out."

"I just remember something," Donna said.

"What's that?" Longarm asked her.

"When I go there to be with heem, I hear the men talk. There is other way out of that cabin. It is secret way."

"Out back through the mountain?"

"I think so."

"Figures," said Longarm. "It's probably a tunnel."

"So what do we do?" asked Ike.

"Blast him out before he gets a chance to use it."

"How you do that?"

"I got all the dynamite I need in a saddlebag Tex willed to me. But I got to get closer."

"How can you do that?"

"Maybe you can lower me down that cliff face onto the cabin's roof."

"That's crazy. You'll get killed."

"Not if you don't let go the rope."

"I will help," said Donna eagerly.

Longarm looked at her and laughed. She was more than eager for him to nail Cheyenne. And it didn't matter how he did it.

"You can, Donna," he told her. "I want you to go up that trail to the cabin and draw Cheyenne out. Tell him I'm willing to let him turn himself in."

"You think he will give himself up? You crazy!"

"I've got to give him the chance. He won't, I know, but that don't matter. I still have to make the offer. And besides, while he's dealing with you, he'll be distracted. The last thing I want is for him to start taking potshots at me while I'm dangling from a rope."

"You will blow me up too!"

"I'll give you plenty of warning."

"We'd better hurry," said Ike. "Cheyenne might pull out any minute."

Longarm nodded, returned to the black, and swung into his saddle. He really wasn't anxious to shimmy down a length of rope to the roof of Cheyenne's cabin carrying a saddlebag packed with dynamite, but he didn't see that he had any reasonable alternative.

Ike snubbed the rope around a solid-looking fir tree and nodded to Longarm. A lighted cheroot clamped between his teeth, Longarm grabbed the rope and swung out over the cliff face, braced his feet against the rock, then proceeded to lower himself toward the cabin roof. Two sticks of dynamite rested in his jacket's side pocket; the rest of the dynamite was in the saddlebag slung over his shoulder.

The drop to the cabin's roof was not a long one—not more than a hundred yards, Longarm estimated. For the past fifteen minutes or so, Cheyenne had remained inside the cabin. The packhorses, heavily laden, were standing over by the barn where the grass was greener and thicker. It appeared that Cheyenne had just about finished loading them up.

As Longarm neared the cabin roof, Donna rode into view and started up the steep trail to the cabin. Almost at once, Longarm heard the cabin door open and saw Cheyenne step out into the front yard, a rifle in his hand.

"What the hell, Donna?" he called down to her. "Where'd you come from?"

"Never mind that," Donna called up to him, pulling the chestnut to a halt. "I got message for you."

"From who?"

"From Longarm. He say you better give up and let him take you in."

"Longarm said that?"

Donna nodded.

"You tryin' to tell me he's alive?" Cheyenne sounded incredulous.

"Yes. He ees alive."

"I don't believe you. That fool lawman's hanging by his neck. He's food for the buzzards."

"I don' think so," said Donna. "I was the one take that noose off his neck."

"*You* did?"

"I did."

"Son of a bitch. I never counted on that."

"So maybe you better give up and let heem take you in."

"You think so, do you."

"Yes," Donna said. Longarm could tell she was having difficulty keeping herself from looking up at him as he dangled in midair over the cabin roof. He increased his speed of descent.

"Okay," Cheyenne told Donna, chuckling meanly. "You go back and tell Longarm I'll give myself up. Tell him to ride on up here and we'll discuss the terms."

At that moment Longarm dropped lightly to the cabin roof. But not lightly enough. At the sound of his boots striking the rooftop, Cheyenne spun, his rifle coming up fast. Longarm flung himself flat on the roof a second before Cheyenne fired.

"Get out of here, Donna!" Longarm cried.

He saw her wheel her horse and with her head down, gallop back down the trail. Certain she was safe, Longarm touched the glowing end of his cheroot to a fuse, then rolled the dynamite lightly off the roof. As it dropped out of sight, he heard the cabin door slam shut. A second later a deafening explosion blew out the front of the cabin, lifting off a section of the roof just in front of Longarm.

Longarm crawled swiftly to the gaping hole and sent another lighted stick of dynamite down into the cabin, then dropped to the ground and lay flat. This time the roof almost lifted off as the second stick of dynamite detonated. After waiting for the smoke to clear, he ducked into the cabin's interior, lugging the saddlebag in with him. Walls were down. Chairs and tables had been reduced to kindling, and small fires flickered in the midst of the smoke-filled ruin.

Longarm kept on through the wreckage, his .44 in one hand, Tex's saddlebag in the other, his lighted cheroot still clamped in his mouth. He pushed into a wrecked hallway and glimpsed a door on the other side of it opening into a smoke-filled room beyond. Pushing into the room, he found himself in a small office built flush against the cliff. As he stepped into it, he saw a heavy door built into the rock wall swing shut and heard running footsteps echoing behind it. Hurrying to the door, he flung it open and found himself at the entrance to a tunnel blasted out of the mountainside. As he peered into the gloom, he glimpsed a light dancing crazily as Cheyenne ran down the tunnel holding a lamp.

Longarm fired at the dancing light. The bullet whined like a maddened hornet as it ricocheted down the tunnel after Cheyenne. The slug came close enough to worry the outlaw, and he halted, blew out the lamp, and returned Longarm's fire.

The slugs whined close past Longarm, one snicking at his coat sleeve. He crouched low and dug into the saddlebag, reminding himself what would happen if one of Cheyenne's rounds struck it. He put the thought out of his mind, touched the glowing end of his cheroot to a fuse, and tossed the dynamite down the tunnel. He saw the stick strike, then roll on, its fuse flickering eerily in the tunnel's stygian night. He heard Cheyenne's sudden oath, and then the sound of the man's boots as he ran on down the tunnel in a desperate bid to outdistance the blast he knew was coming.

Longarm sent another stick of dynamite after the first—this one with a shorter fuse—then turned and dove back out through the heavy door, pushing it shut behind him. A second later the titanic double blast came, the force of it blowing the door open wide and filling the small room with rock dust and debris. So terrific was the detonation Longarm could hear the walls inside the tunnel collapsing, causing great puffs of smoke and debris to pulse out through the doorway. Coughing, his eyes searing from the smoke, Longarm ran from the cabin, aware that its ceiling beams, weakened by the explosions, might collapse at any moment.

160

As soon as he was clear of the cabin, he lay Tex's saddlebag down, then looked up at Ike on the top of the cliff. He waved to him, then beckoned to him to come down and bring Longarm's horse. He saw Ike wave in return, then move back off the top of the cliff to get the black.

Longarm looked around then and saw that the packhorses, obviously spooked by the dynamite blasts, were huddled together beside the barn, their eyes wild, their tails flicking nervously. He was walking over to gentle them down when he heard Donna's scream. He turned back to the trail and saw Cheyenne, astride Donna's chestnut, galloping away through the ravine. Somehow, he had escaped the blasts. Without a horse, Longarm could not give chase. And he had left his rifle in his saddle sling.

He saw Donna stagger into view, and a moment later Cheyenne slipped to one side in the saddle, then tumbled loosely from the horse. Longarm ran down the long trail, catching up to Donna in the ravine. She had a nasty welt on her left cheekbone and her eyes were smoldering with anger, but aside from that she appeared to be uninjured. From her vantage point on the floor of the ravine, unlike Longarm, she had not seen Cheyenne topple from her horse.

"That son of a bitch!" she cried, rushing up to Cheyenne. "He come out of the rocks before I know it and pull me off my horse."

"Don't worry. He didn't get far. I saw him fall from the saddle."

"Hah!" she cried, exultant. "I know that when I see heem!"

161

"He's hurt bad, is he?"

"You blow him up!"

"Let's go. He's not far."

When they came upon Cheyenne, he had crawled to a boulder and was sitting up with his back to it. The moment Longarm and Donna came in sight, he flung up his six-gun and fired at them.

Longarm pulled Donna down behind a boulder and took out his .44. Then he peered carefully at Cheyenne. The outlaw still held his revolver, but he didn't look capable of doing much with it. Longarm doubted if the man would even be able to raise it again.

Donna was right.

Cheyenne had not escaped the effects of that titanic blast. His left arm hung lifelessly from his shoulder and a ragged piece had been ripped out of one side of his face. His left leg was a bloody, splintered fragment of shinbone. How he had managed to ride this far was a mystery to Longarm.

"You're finished, Cheyenne," Longarm called. "Give it up. Surrender."

Amazingly, Cheyenne lifted his revolver and fired at Longarm—or rather, in Longarm's general direction. He didn't aim. He just fired. And fired. Until the hammer came down on an empty chamber. Then he flung the gun aside and leaning his head back against the boulder, waited.

Longarm got to his feet. Donna also. They walked over to where the still-conscious outlaw lay and gazed down at him. His one remaining eye shifted in the man's shattered visage and what passed for a smile crossed it.

"You got me, you bastard," Cheyenne said, his voice barely audible. "Now do me a favor. Finish me off. Please."

Longarm thought of Sam Calder then—and of the pleasure Cheyenne had taken in the contemplation of Longarm's imminent hanging. He had not shot Sam Calder in the gut by mistake. He had done it on purpose, relishing the cruel death he had thus inflicted on a man who had once saved his life. Donna was only partly right. Cheyenne was a devil, yes—but he was also a man who killed for pleasure and without a shred of remorse.

Longarm glanced up at the sky. There were no buzzards circling yet. But there would be soon enough, and if fate were kind, the Cheyenne Kid would be able to hear the flutter of their wings before he felt the tearing pain of their sharp, obscene beaks.

He turned away from Cheyenne and taking Donna's arm, led her away from the fallen outlaw.

Chapter 12

When Longarm and Donna got back to what was left of Cheyenne's cabin, Ike was nowhere in sight, but his horse and the black were grazing alongside the two pack-horses. It looked as if the presence of the two saddle horses had calmed down the packhorses nicely.

Longarm was walking, while Donna rode the chest-nut. Halting in front of the cabin, Longarm realized that Ike must be prowling around somewhere in the cabin's wreckage. Considering the condition of the structure, that was not a very healthy idea.

"Ike!" he called.

The old mountain man appeared in the ragged hole that had once been the cabin's doorway.

"What the hell are you doing in there?" Longarm asked him.

"What do you think? I'm looking for Cheyenne's gold."

Donna jumped down from the chestnut and started

eagerly toward the cabin. But Longarm grabbed her and would not let her proceed. Furious, she turned on him.

"Let me go!"

"Don't go in there," he told her. "It's too dangerous. The rest of that cabin might collapse at any minute."

"No, it will not do that," she insisted, pulling free of Longarm's grasp.

"You can't be sure."

"I don't care!" she told him, starting once more for the cabin. "There is much gold in there! Many bags. I see them myself. I remember."

"Ike," Longarm said. "Maybe that gold dust is stashed on one of these packhorses."

"I already checked them both," Ike replied. "There's no gold on either horse."

With a weary shrug, Longarm followed Donna toward the cabin, and then joined the two of them as they entered the wrecked cabin. Since Donna remembered where Cheyenne stored his valuables, they followed her straight back to the cliff wall and into the same room from which Cheyenne had gained entrance to the escape tunnel. There was a gaping hole in the roof, and what Longarm had not noticed before in his eagerness to overtake Cheyenne was now in plain sight. Beside a tall file cabinet in one corner sat a huge safe. Debris from the ceiling and one collapsed wall covered everything. One beam had crashed down, slamming into the file cabinet and crushing it into the wall. Beside it, the safe stood unscathed, a thick layer of rock dust covering it.

And its massive door was wide open.

"He took the gold dust!" Donna cried.

Ike said, "That means he had it when he entered that escape tunnel."

"But he had nothing when I see heem," Donna cried.

Longarm went to the tunnel entrance and peered into the rubble-filled interior. Cheyenne had been carrying the gold dust when he fled. He must have put it down when he doused the lamp and fired back at Longarm. At the sight of the dynamite rolling toward him, its lighted fuse sputtering, he had left the gold dust and run for his life.

But not fast enough.

Beside him, Donna and Ike stared into the rubble-filled escape tunnel.

"The gold dust is in there still," Ike said, "where Cheyenne must have left it."

"If so," Longarm reminded him, "the bags have been blown to bits and the gold dust is back where it came from—under a mountain of dirt and rock."

"What do you mean, back where it belongs?" asked Ike.

"I'll leave that to you," Longarm replied. "You're the philosopher."

Donna took a deep sigh. "I guess now I go back to Timber City."

"And I'll return to my place," said Ike. He looked at Donna then and smiled. "You can visit me any time you want, Donna."

"You have no money, old man."

"But I have hundreds of books. There's true wealth in them."

"But no gold."

"No gold."

167

The three left the cabin, and as they rode off with the packhorses, Longarm tossed one last stick of dynamite into the cabin's wreckage, reducing it to rubble.

Rose was in a corner of the saloon, one arm around the shoulder of a porcine fellow in a bowler hat who was slobbering drunkenly over a beer. She was as pale as death, thinner than he had remembered her, and there was a look in her eyes that told him only a very small part of her was still truly alive, still capable of hope.

She didn't see him until he was almost to her table. When she did, she straightened up so swiftly, she might have been slapped.

"My God, it's you," she said, her voice hushed.

"Surprised?"

"I never thought I'd see you again."

"I told you I'd stop by on my way back. You still want to go with me?"

"You mean back to Jack."

"That's right. Your husband Jack. And his ranch."

She did not hesitate for an instant. "Yes. I do."

"How soon can you leave?"

She looked down at the fellow sitting at the table with her and pulled her arm away from his heavy shoulder. He made a clumsy grab for her and she slapped his hand away.

"Now," she said. "Right this minute."

"No. Tomorrow morning's soon enough. I've had a long day in the saddle and I want to get into a good hot tub and sleep on a bed tonight. I'm staying at the hotel. I'll see you in the lobby first thing in the morning."

"I'll be there."

"Good."

He turned to leave the saloon.

"Longarm . . . ?"

He halted and looked back at her.

"Do you think Jack will still be there?"

He saw in her face her sudden, terrified concern that she would return to nothing—only an empty cabin in the middle of a desolate wilderness. It was a possibility, he realized.

"There's only one way to find out," he told her, and continued on out of the saloon.

Longarm was surprised at how much better the ranch looked. The stumps that had pocked the front yard had been pulled out, and a scythe had been used to good effect all around the cabin, transforming the weeds and tall grass into a lawn. The henhouse looked new, and the chickens were neatly and effectively fenced in with bright new wire. The barn had been painted a good solid gray color, and the chinks in the cabin's logs had been filled with clay. There were even panes of glass in all the windows, and a sturdy, recently constructed veranda ran the length of the cabin. And most remarkable of all, the roof was shingled.

As Longarm and Rose rode into the front yard, a clean-shaven fellow in bib overalls came out to greet them. He had a bright, inquisitive face, blue eyes, and a smile he could not keep from using.

"Welcome, strangers," he said. "Light and set a spell. I got fresh coffee on the stove and doughnuts I made fresh this morning."

"Sounds great," said Longarm, dismounting. "My

name's Long, and this here is Rose."

"Frank Bidderman," the man replied, stepping closer to shake Longarm's hand. Taking it, Longarm found the man's clasp as hearty as his smile.

Longarm helped Rose down off her horse. While he did so, she kept staring in amazement first at the ranch house and then at the fellow who had just stepped out through the doorway of a cabin that had once belonged to her husband.

"This your place, Frank?" Longarm inquired casually.

"Yep. Won it in a poker game a couple of weeks back. Best hand I ever had. Three aces, two kings. I also won enough to fix the place up some. Now all I need is a good woman to keep me honest."

Rose cleared her throat nervously. "What happened to that feller you won the place from?"

"Jack Collins? Oh, the poor son of a bitch got himself shot to death a couple of days later. He was drunk as a lord and insulted a bar girl. She killed him with a belly gun. He was a man sure knew how to find bad luck."

"I can smell that coffee from here," Longarm said, and with a nod to Rose, let her precede him into the cabin.

When Longarm left three days later, Frank Bidderman and Rose stood in the doorway, waving good-bye. Rose had come home and Bidderman had found a woman who would keep him honest.

Longarm had never, as a rule, believed in miracles, but after this he decided he would keep an open mind on the subject.

Fury knew something was wrong long before he saw the wagon train spread out, unmoving, across the plains in front of him.

From miles away, he had noticed the cloud of dust kicked up by the hooves of the mules and oxen pulling the wagons. Then he had seen that tan-colored pall stop and gradually be blown away by the ceaseless prairie wind.

It was the middle of the afternoon, much too early for a wagon train to be stopping for the day. Now, as Fury topped a small, grass-covered ridge and saw the motionless wagons about half a mile away, he wondered just what kind of damn fool was in charge of the train.

Stopping out in the open without even forming into a circle was like issuing an invitation to the Sioux, the Cheyenne, or the Pawnee. War parties roamed these plains all the time just looking for a situation as tempting as this one.

Fury reined in, leaned forward in his saddle, and thought about it. Nothing said he had to go help those pilgrims. They might not even want his help.

But from the looks of things, they needed his help, whether they wanted it or not.

He heeled the rangy lineback dun into a trot toward the wagons. As he approached, he saw figures scurrying back and forth around the canvas-topped vehicles. Looked sort of like an anthill after you stomp it.

Fury pulled the dun to a stop about twenty feet from the lead wagon. Near it a man was stretched out on the ground with so many men and women gathered around him that Fury could only catch a glimpse of him through the crowd. When some of the men turned to look at him, Fury said, "Howdy. Thought it looked like you were having trouble."

"Damn right, mister," one of the pilgrims snapped. "And if you're of a mind to give us more, I'd advise against it."

Fury crossed his hands on the saddlehorn and shifted in the saddle, easing his tired muscles. "I'm not looking to cause trouble for anybody," he said mildly.

He supposed he might appear a little threatening to a bunch of immigrants who had never been any farther west than the Mississippi. Several days had passed since his face had known the touch of the razor, and his rough-hewn features could be a little intimidating even without the beard stubble. Besides that, he was well armed with a Colt's Third Model Dragoon pistol holstered on his right hip, a Bowie knife sheathed on his left, and a Sharps carbine in a saddleboot under his right thigh. And he had the look of a man who knew how to use all three weapons.

A husky, broad-shouldered six-footer, John Fury's height was apparent even on horseback. He wore a broad-brimmed, flat-crowned black hat, a blue work shirt, and fringed buckskin pants that were tucked into high-topped black boots. As he swung down from the saddle, a man's voice, husky with strain, called out, "Who's that? Who are you?"

The crowd parted, and Fury got a better look at the figure on the ground. It was obvious that he was the one who had spoken. There was blood on the man's face, and from the twisted look of him as he lay on the ground, he was busted up badly inside.

Fury let the dun's reins trail on the ground, confident that the horse wouldn't go anywhere. He walked over to the injured man and crouched beside him. "Name's John Fury," he said.

The man's breath hissed between his teeth, whether in pain or surprise Fury couldn't have said. "Fury? I heard of you."

Fury just nodded. Quite a few people reacted that way when they heard his name.

"I'm . . . Leander Crofton. Wagonmaster of . . . this here train." The man struggled to speak. He appeared to be in his fifties and had a short, grizzled beard and the leathery skin of a man who had spent nearly his whole life outdoors. His pale blue eyes were narrowed in a permanent squint.

"What happened to you?" Fury asked.

"It was a terrible accident—" began one of the men standing nearby, but he fell silent when Fury cast a hard glance at him. Fury had asked Crofton, and that was who he looked toward for the answer.

Crofton smiled a little, even though it cost him an effort. "Pulled a damn fool stunt," he said. "Horse nearly stepped on a rattler, and I let it rear up and get away from me. Never figured the critter'd spook so easy." The wagonmaster paused to draw a breath. The air rattled in his throat and chest. "Tossed me off and stomped all over me. Not the first time I been stepped on by a horse, but then a couple of the oxen pullin' the lead wagon got me, too, 'fore the driver could get 'em stopped."

"God forgive me, I . . . I am so sorry." The words came in a tortured voice from a small man with dark curly hair and a beard. He was looking down at Crofton with lines of misery etched onto his face.

"Wasn't your fault, Leo," Crofton said. "Just . . . bad luck."

Fury had seen men before who had been trampled by horses. Crofton was in a bad way, and Fury could tell by the look in the man's eyes that Crofton was well aware of it. The wagonmaster's chances were pretty slim.

"Mind if I look you over?" Fury asked. Maybe he could do something to make Crofton's passing a little easier, anyway.

One of the other men spoke before Crofton had a chance to answer. "Are you a doctor, sir?" he asked.

Fury glanced up at him, saw a slender, middle-aged man with iron-gray hair. "No, but I've patched up quite a few hurt men in my time."

"Well, I am a doctor," the gray-haired man said. "And I'd appreciate it if you wouldn't try to move or examine

Mr. Crofton. I've already done that, and I've given him some laudanum to ease the pain."

Fury nodded. He had been about to suggest a shot of whiskey, but the laudanum would probably work better.

Crofton's voice was already slower and more drowsy from the drug as he said, "Fury . . ."

"Right here."

"I got to be sure about something . . . You said your name was . . . John Fury."

"That's right."

"The same John Fury who . . . rode with Fremont and Kit Carson?"

"I know them," Fury said simply.

"And had a run-in with Cougar Johnson in Santa Fe?"

"Yes."

"Traded slugs with Hemp Collier in San Antone last year?"

"He started the fight, didn't give me much choice but to finish it."

"Thought so." Crofton's hand lifted and clutched weakly at Fury's sleeve. "You got to . . . make me a promise."

Fury didn't like the sound of that. Promises made to dying men usually led to a hell of a lot of trouble.

Crofton went on, "You got to give me . . . your word . . . that you'll take these folks through . . . to where they're goin'."

"I'm no wagonmaster," Fury said.

"You know the frontier," Crofton insisted. Anger gave him strength, made him rally enough to lift his head from

179

the ground and glare at Fury. "You can get 'em through. I know you can."

"Don't excite him," warned the gray-haired doctor.

"Why the hell not?" Fury snapped, glancing up at the physician. He noticed now that the man had his arm around the shoulders of a pretty red-headed girl in her teens, probably his daughter. He went on, "What harm's it going to do?"

The girl exclaimed, "Oh! How can you be so . . . so callous?"

Crofton said, "Fury's just bein' practical, Carrie. He knows we got to . . . got to hash this out now. Only chance we'll get." He looked at Fury again. "I can't make you promise, but it . . . it'd sure set my mind at ease while I'm passin' over if I knew you'd take care of these folks."

Fury sighed. It was rare for him to promise anything to anybody. Giving your word was a quick way of getting in over your head in somebody else's problems. But Crofton was dying, and even though they had never crossed paths before, Fury recognized in the old man a fellow Westerner.

"All right," he said.

A little shudder ran through Crofton's battered body, and he rested his head back against the grassy ground. "Thanks," he said, the word gusting out of him along with a ragged breath.

"Where are you headed?" Fury figured the immigrants could tell him, but he wanted to hear the destination from Crofton.

"Colorado Territory . . . Folks figure to start 'em a town . . . somewhere on the South Platte. Won't be hard for you to find . . . a good place."

No, it wouldn't, Fury thought. No wagon train journey could be called easy, but at least this one wouldn't have to deal with crossing mountains, just prairie.

Prairie filled with savages and outlaws, that is.

A grim smile plucked at Fury's mouth as that thought crossed his mind. "Anything else you need to tell me?" he asked Crofton.

The wagonmaster shook his head and let his eyelids slide closed. "Nope. Figger I'll rest a spell now. We can talk again later."

"Sure," Fury said softly, knowing that in all likelihood, Leander Crofton would never wake up from this rest.

Less than a minute later, Crofton coughed suddenly, a wracking sound. His head twisted to the side, and blood welled for a few seconds from the corner of his mouth. Fury heard some of the women in the crowd cry out and turn away, and he suspected some of the men did, too.

"Well, that's all," he said, straightening easily from his kneeling position beside Crofton's body. He looked at the doctor. The red-headed teenager had her face pressed to the front of her father's shirt and her shoulders were shaking with sobs. She wasn't the only one crying, and even the ones who were dry-eyed still looked plenty grim.

"We'll have a funeral service as soon as a grave is dug," said the doctor. "Then I suppose we'll be moving on. You should know, Mr. . . . Fury, was it? You should know that none of us will hold you to that promise you made to Mr. Crofton."

Fury shrugged. "Didn't ask if you intended to or

181

not. I'm the one who made the promise. Reckon I'll keep it."

He saw surprise on some of the faces watching him. All of these travelers had probably figured him for some sort of drifter. Well, that was fair enough. Drifting was what he did best.

But that didn't mean he was a man who ignored promises. He had given his word, and there was no way he could back out now.

He met the startled stare of the doctor and went on, "Who's the captain here? You?"

"No, I . . . You see, we hadn't gotten around to electing a captain yet. We only left Independence a couple of weeks ago, and we were all happy with the leadership of Mr. Crofton. We didn't see the need to select a captain."

Crofton should have insisted on it, Fury thought with a grimace. You never could tell when trouble would pop up. Crofton's body lying on the ground was grisly proof of that.

Fury looked around at the crowd. From the number of people standing there, he figured most of the wagons in the train were at least represented in this gathering. Lifting his voice, he said, "You all heard what Crofton asked me to do. I gave him my word I'd take over this wagon train and get it on through to Colorado Territory. Anybody got any objection to that?"

His gaze moved over the faces of the men and women who were standing and looking silently back at him. The silence was awkward and heavy. No one was objecting, but Fury could tell they weren't too happy with this unexpected turn of events.

Well, he thought, when he had rolled out of his soogans that morning, he hadn't expected to be in charge of a wagon train full of strangers before the day was over.

The gray-haired doctor was the first one to find his voice. "We can't speak for everyone on the train, Mr. Fury," he said. "But I don't know you, sir, and I have some reservations about turning over the welfare of my daughter and myself to a total stranger."

Several others in the crowd nodded in agreement with the sentiment expressed by the physician.

"Crofton knew me."

"He knew you have a reputation as some sort of gunman!"

Fury took a deep breath and wished to hell he had come along after Crofton was already dead. Then he wouldn't be saddled with a pledge to take care of these people.

"I'm not wanted by the law," he said. "That's more than a lot of men out here on the frontier can say, especially those who have been here for as long as I have. Like I said, I'm not looking to cause trouble. I was riding along and minding my own business when I came across you people. There's too many of you for me to fight. You want to start out toward Colorado on your own, I can't stop you. But you're going to have to learn a hell of a lot in a hurry."

"What do you mean by that?"

Fury smiled grimly. "For one thing, if you stop spread out like this, you're making a target of yourselves for every Indian in these parts who wants a few fresh scalps for his lodge." He looked pointedly at the long red hair of the doctor's daughter. Carrie—that was what Crofton had called her, Fury remembered.

Her father paled a little, and another man said, "I didn't think there was any Indians this far east." Other murmurs of concern came from the crowd.

Fury knew he had gotten through to them. But before any of them had a chance to say that he should honor his promise to Crofton and take over, the sound of hoofbeats made him turn quickly.

A man was riding hard toward the wagon train from the west, leaning over the neck of his horse and urging it on to greater speed. The brim of his hat was blown back by the wind of his passage, and Fury saw anxious, dark brown features underneath it. The newcomer galloped up to the crowd gathered next to the lead wagon, hauled his lathered mount to a halt, and dropped lithely from the saddle. His eyes went wide with shock when he saw Crofton's body on the ground, and then his gaze flicked to Fury.

"You son of a bitch!" he howled.

And his hand darted toward the gun holstered on his hip.

If you enjoyed this book, subscribe now and get...

TWO FREE

A $7.00 VALUE—

If you would like to read more of the very best, most exciting, adventurous, action-packed Westerns being published today, you'll want to subscribe to True Value's Western Home Subscription Service.

Each month the editors of True Value will select the 6 very best Westerns from America's leading publishers for special readers like you. You'll be able to preview these new titles as soon as they are published, *FREE* for ten days with no obligation!

TWO FREE BOOKS

When you subscribe, we'll send you your first month's shipment of the newest and best 6 Westerns for you to preview. With your first shipment, two of these books will be yours as our introductory gift to you absolutely *FREE* (a $7.00 value), regardless of what you decide to do. If

you like them, as much as we think you will, keep all six books but pay for just 4 at the low subscriber rate of just $2.75 each. If you decide to return them, keep 2 of the titles as our gift. No obligation.

Special Subscriber Savings

When you become a True Value subscriber you'll save money several ways. First, all regular monthly selections will be billed at the low subscriber price of just $2.75 each. That's at least a savings of $4.50 each month below the publishers price. Second, there is never any shipping, handling or other hidden charges—*Free home delivery*. What's more there is no minimum number of books you must buy, you may return any selection for full credit and you can cancel your subscription at any time. A TRUE VALUE!